My Lord Rogue

A Nelson's Tea Novella

BY
Katherine Bone

My Lord Rogue
Copyright © 2018 by Katherine Bone
Published by Seas the Day Publishing
(Second Edition)
Cover Design by For the Muse Designs
Editing by Double Vision Editorial

All rights reserved. No part of this book may be reproduced in any form by any electronic or mechanical means—except in the case of brief quotations embedded in critical articles or reviews—without the author's written permission.

The characters and events portrayed in this book are fictitious. Any similarity to real persons, living or dead, is purely coincidental and not intended by the author.

For more information contact katherine@katherinebone.com
or visit www.katherinebone.com.

Also Available

―――

The Regent's Revenge Series

―――

The Pirate's Duchess, Novella
The Pirate's Debt, Book #2
The Pirate's Duty, Book #3

―――

The Heart of a Hero Series

―――

The Mercenary Pirate

―――

The Nelson's Tea Series

―――

Duke by Day, Rogue by Night, Book #2, Coming Soon

Dedication

"Desperate affairs require desperate measures."
~ *Admiral Lord Horatio Nelson*

To M.V. Freeman, Crystal R. Lee, and my family for encouraging and inspiring my stories. Dreams really do come true!

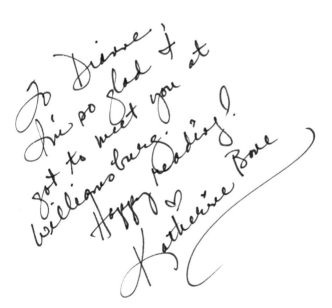

Prologue

Kent
October 1801

"THEY SAY THEY'LL invade us these terrible foe. They frighten our women, our children, our beaus, but if should their flat-bottoms, in darkness set oar, still Britons they'll find to receive them on shore." The sun moved behind a cloud as Gillian Corbet, Baroness Chauncey sang "Heart of Oak" and bent to snip several clumps of heather from a plant in her garden.

The vibrant colors of the flowers she'd grown, combined with their floral scents, reminded her of her tenure on stage at the Theatre Royal, Drury Lane when wealthy benefactors would gift her bouquets. The memory of one admirer in particular held extraordinary power over her—Lord Simon Danbury, the second son of the third Duke of Throckmorton. Tall, honorable, and regretfully betrothed to another, he'd been a patron of the arts and her first love. Smiling at the memory, no longer angry or distraught about the separate paths their lives had taken, Gillian cut a dozen bloodred roses for the arrangement she was preparing for the foyer.

Five years had passed since her husband had assumed the name Lucien Corbet, Baron Chauncey after escaping the guillotine in France. Lucien was a "Chouan," a follower of Jean and René Cottereau's revolution against tyranny and a descendant of pamphleteers. They were a team, she and he, bent on weakening Napoleon's power as master spies.

Lucien had recruited Gillian to the rebellion after their arranged marriage. She'd taught him the art of disguise, while he'd taught her the art of subterfuge. As operatives in England's employ—Gillian often pretending to be a widow—she and Lucien strove to stop Napoleon's secret police while appearing to be self-absorbed members of the *ton*. Together, they'd transformed a dilapidated mansion with its forgotten garden into a haven for butterflies and hummingbirds, and a place of sanctuary to which they could return after dangerous missions.

A clatter of horse's hooves interrupted her musings. *Lucien!*

Gillian rose excitedly, abandoning her roses, and sheltered her eyes from the sun. She'd had misgivings about Lucien traveling to France without her, and it pleased her to know he'd safely returned.

But wait . . .

She squinted, certain she was mistaken. But there it was again: a riderless horse galloping pell-mell to the house. As the black horse neared, the white star-shaped marking on its chest became clear. This was not just any horse, but Lucien's. Her heart sank.

"Polaris!" She dropped her basket of flowers and picked up her skirts, trampling the garden in her haste to intercept the beast. There was only one reason Polaris would return without Lucien. He was in trouble!

Polaris's nostrils flared as he stamped the ground before her, his eyes wild. "Where is he?" she asked the magnificent horse when she finally got him to stop kicking.

Polaris shook his head, laboring to tell her something he didn't have the capacity to say. Dread seized Gillian's heart. She searched the horse for signs of injury, anything that would indicate what had happened to her husband. Lucien's untouched musket was still sheathed behind the saddle. Whatever had happened, he had not been given the chance to retrieve the weapon. *An ambush?*

Nausea washed over her. She grabbed the reins and circled Polaris so she could mount him. Blood coated the black's thick mane, and she brought the reins around and stepped up to the saddle. Gillian bit her lip, refusing to think the worst, as she touched the sticky strands to gauge how far away Lucien could be.

Still warm.

Lucien must have sent his horse to her directly after being attacked.

"Take me to him," she ordered.

With her heart beating frantically, she wheeled Polaris southward and kicked the horse's flanks, urging him into a run back the way he'd come. She and Lucien had been through plenty of hellish scrapes together in their five years of marriage, and she wasn't a fool. She knew what this meant. And as she'd been trained to do, she girded herself for what she might find as Polaris's gallop took them past hedgerow fences. Time seemed to drag on as they raced up a hill and over a stream before Polaris transitioned to a canter, and then ambled to a stop. He raised his head and snorted violently.

Nerves on edge, Gillian knew Lucien was somewhere nearby. She slipped out of the saddle and landed softly on her feet, careful not to make another sound as she took in her surroundings. When nothing alerted her to Lucien's presence, she walked along the edge of the wood until she located a trail of blood leading into the trees. She stopped, her heart thumping faster.

Leaves rustled. An eerie silence met her ears until she heard the faint cry of a tawny owl—the signal Lucien had adopted from the Chouans. He was close, hiding, but in danger of being discovered. Her hopes ignited. Whoever was searching for her husband intended to finish him off, which meant she still had time to stop Lucien's attacker.

A twig snapped fifty paces away in the thicket. Then another.

Gillian hiked her skirts up and secured them about her knees with straps she'd sewn into her gown, and then she pulled the loaded musket out of its sheath on Polaris's back. She crept into the forest, careful to step only where her kid leather boots would be less likely to make noise. The last thing she wanted to do was announce her presence. She couldn't help Lucien if she were dead.

"*Vous ne pouvez pas fuir,*" a deep voice shouted in French. "You cannot run."

The threat came from the northwest and thirty feet off her position. Someone had followed Lucien, most likely someone who also planned not to leave any witnesses behind, which explained why her husband had not ridden directly to the house for help. He'd ventured to France this time at the behest of Vice-Admiral Lord Horatio Nelson and Henry Dundas, the prime minister's former war secretary. Lucien had proven that as a Frenchman and Jacobin with influential political ties, he would not be intimidated by Napoleon's secret police.

A gun cocked somewhere beyond the trees to her left. Laughter, maniacal and victorious, met her ears. She instantly reacted, sneaking toward the sound, aiming the musket at anything that moved as she tried to anticipate where her quarry would emerge.

There.

Through the trees, she caught sight of a man. Tall and blond, he was dressed in black and towered over someone. He held a gun in his hand. "You led a merry chase, Corbet."

Gillian gasped. *Lucien!*

Filled with urgency, she fired the musket. Her aim was

true, and the man jerked, twisted, and fired his weapon into the air as he fell dead. Nausea coiled inside her. She'd been trained to kill, but she'd never been forced to do so. Lucien had always been there to protect her. And now, if anyone else was looking for her husband, the assassin had made their whereabouts known.

Fearing for their lives, Gillian ran as fast as she could through the thicket, paying no heed to the branches clawing at her legs as she made her way down the hill to her husband. When she arrived at the scene, she found him laboring to breathe beneath his attacker's dead weight.

"Gillian." His voice held none of his usual vigor, frightening her all the more.

"Don't move!" she cried. She grabbed the stranger's legs and hauled his body off her husband. When Lucien was freed, she dropped to her knees beside him and lowered her startled gaze to his bloody hands. They were clasped over his stomach. He peeled his hands away, revealing a gaping wound that confirmed her suspicions. He would not survive this time. Her breath caught in her chest. "No. No. No. I refuse to believe it. This cannot be happening."

"My luck has run out, *mon amour*," he said. "I've lost too much blood. I don't—" he inhaled deeply "—have much time."

She had to get him home. She had herbs, potions, and ways of dealing with injuries there. Surely ... "You are not going to die!" she vowed. "Polaris and I will take you home." She started to rise, but he grabbed her by the arm, stopping her. She frowned as she glanced down at his loose grip. Where was his strength?

He couldn't be dying.

Fighting back tears, she sank to her knees. *Five years!* That's all they'd had together. It had not been enough time to learn to love each other the way a husband and wife should.

"I will bandage your wound," she said, struggling to rip strips of fabric from the hem of her skirts. "I must stop the bleeding. You will be fine, Husband. We have been through worse. You will be fine," she repeated. "You will see."

"Stop," he pleaded weakly, pulling her closer so he could whisper in her ear. "No . . . time. Nelson . . . in . . . danger."

She pulled back and stared down at him. "Admiral Nelson?"

"*Oui*. He has returned to London. He is . . . unwell—another bout of malaria. They plan—" he coughed up blood "—to strike in two days' time at Drury Lane." She dabbed his mouth. "Must stop . . . Fouché."

Joseph Fouché was Napoleon's chief of police. If he was involved, the stakes were incredibly high.

"D'Auvergne," Lucien continued. "He said . . . head wounds Hadfield received . . . Battle of Tourcoing . . . conditioned him . . . to kill the king."

Her eyes widened. This would mean Fouché had been at the heart of the assassination attempt on King George at Drury Lane a year ago.

"It all makes sense . . . now." Lucien tightened his grip. "You must help the admiral . . ."

"I cannot go back there." She shook her head. "What you ask—"

"No choice, *ma chérie*." He smiled wanly, touching her cheek with his cold, sticky hand. "Nelson needs . . . you. Go to Stanton."

"The marquess?" They had trained Percival Avery, the Marquess of Stanton, to be a spy. They'd worked together and become close friends.

"*Oui*. He will know what to do . . ." Lucien spasmed, and his pain-racked groan tore through her defenses.

"No." She squeezed his hand and held it to her lips. "You will go with me, Lucien." She turned her cheek, untold agony slicing through her as she was struck by how deeply she truly loved her husband. It was not the all-encompassing love she'd felt for Lord Danbury, but it was comfortable, reliable, and lasting.

His eyes turned glassy. "We've shared many things... but never what you needed most, *ma chérie*. Go to him."

He spoke of Danbury now, and she knew it. But deep in her heart she also knew she couldn't love a man who'd married another. "You are wrong," she cried. But he wasn't and that hurt the most. "I *have* loved you, Lucien."

In my own way.

"And I you," he said. Blood trickled out of his mouth, and she dabbed his lips again, praying that God would spare his life. "Promise me... you will stop... Fouché. The admiral must... assemble Nelson's Tea."

She squeezed his hand and tried to soothe him, stroking his forehead. She nodded, tears spilling out of her eyes. "I promise." She gripped Lucien's cold, clammy hand tightly to her breast. "I will promise you anything."

"Good." He writhed in pain, struggling wildly, but somehow the force of his will allowed him to form coherent thoughts. He inhaled loudly, a gruff rattling that dug into Gillian, never to be forgotten. "They plan... kill Nelson... when arrives... Holcroft's play..."

Tears fell from her eyes as she wiped more blood from his face, this time off his chin. "You speak of Holcroft's *Deaf and Dumb*?"

"*Oui*... Be there... the marquess..." Lucien squeezed her hand almost violently as another spasm overtook him.

"I will find Stanton," she vowed. "I will do whatever it takes."

He struggled to place something in her hand. "Here... this... explains."

"You have my word," she said, fisting the crumpled missive in her palm. "I will not fail you, my dearest love."

"My love." He smiled faintly and closed his eyes.

Unchecked tears slowly streamed down Gillian's face and a sob tore from her throat. "Lucien, no . . ."

A twig snapped. Then another, the sound moving closer in the woods.

She searched the trees before looking back down at her husband. "Someone is coming."

"Leave," he said. "Now. I beg . . ."

"No." Tears escaped her eyes as she shook her head. "How can you ask such a thing?"

Voices, faint but growing more audible, carried through the trees. She glanced at the dead man's gun that had drawn his companions. By all that was holy, what was she supposed to do now?

Lucien arched his back and tightened his grip. "Go," he said more forcefully. "Warn them." It was an order she'd be foolish not to accept.

Her heart pounded against her chest as her gaze darted around the perimeter. If she didn't get her husband up now, they wouldn't be able to escape.

"I will not leave without you," she whispered. "Get up. Fight to live."

His body grew lax, and his lush, velvety-brown eyes drank her in. "You have pretended . . . to be a widow." He gasped. Blood trickled out of his mouth. "No need to pretend . . . now . . ."

One

*"All the world's a stage,
And all the men and women merely players . . ."*
~William Shakespeare, As You Like It

Westminster
Two days later

GILLIAN CORBET STRAIGHTENED her shoulders, adjusted her black veil, and entered the lion's den, willingly taking a step toward her own destruction. She had not returned to Drury Lane since falling in love with Lord Simon Danbury, the man whose kiss had promised her happiness, and then finding out he was marrying another. Now, after what seemed like a lifetime of heartbreak and renewal, she was a widow in the truest sense. No need to call upon her acting skills now. Not when she felt Lucien's loss so keenly and carried the weight of the world on her shoulders. The stakes of Vice-Admiral Nelson's impending assassination would be an incomprehensible blow to her husband's legacy, the monarchy, the Admiralty, and England. The death of England's savior would weaken British morale at a time when war was already threatening the country's shores. She could not allow it. She *would* not allow it. She'd promised Lucien she would prevent such a catastrophe, or she'd die in the process of fulfilling her vow.

Britain depended on a network of spies to outwit the enemy, and the one thing she had in her favor was that her husband had trained her well. Failure was never an option. And she would do anything to honor Lucien's dying wish, even if Lord Danbury discovered her presence. Lord Danbury was a member of the *ton* and one of Nelson's most respected allies. After marrying Lucien, Gillian had also learned that Danbury was a member of British counterintelligence. She shivered. In the five years they'd been together, Lucien had only requested one thing: never tell Danbury that she'd been recruited as a spy.

If Lucien was right, the audience at the Theatre Royal, Drury Lane would get more than they had bargained for at tonight's performance of Holcroft's *Deaf and Dumb*. The play gave attendees a chance to meet—or at least see—the Baron of the Nile, Vice-Admiral Lord Horatio Nelson himself, who had recently returned from India with his mistress, Lady Emma Hamilton, wife of Sir William Hamilton. It was rumored that the three of them were involved in a tryst, that she had delivered the vice-admiral a child—a daughter—in January.

A sense of urgency embraced Gillian as she inspected the overeager throng within Drury Lane's box lobby.

"I'm told the admiral's health is failing," said a nearby woman, fanning herself with a hand-painted fan in the entryway.

"Malaria," the man to her left responded. "Came down with it again, they say. But he won't see *her*."

"Who?" the woman asked, glancing up at him.

"His wife." The woman's face brightened, and her brows shot up as he grimaced. "Lady Nelson deserves respect," he scolded. "It's repugnant the way he parades that Hamilton woman about."

Gillian groaned inwardly, remembering the ghastly moment she'd suggested being Danbury's mistress once she'd found out he was betrothed. He'd softly told her that he loved her, and because he loved her, he wouldn't allow it. He'd explained that she deserved to be treated like a queen, not a man's bird of paradise.

Much about Nelson's troubled marriage was in the public domain, though Frances Nisbet Nelson—the rightful *Lady* Nelson—was continuously held in the highest regard, no matter how goatish her husband behaved.

Above Gillian, crystal chandeliers lit the box lobby, illuminating the grand amphitheater and casting an ethereal glow on the well-to-do and sundry congregating in the horseshoe-shaped audience. Ladies in attendance clustered together. Men slapped one another on the back. The splendorous decor accentuated the figures of the silken beauties and the laced cuffs, brightly polished uniforms, and tailored suits of men sporting starched cravats. A spectacular promenade of actors and audience alike heralded a night of jovial bliss, contradicting the pulsing sense of desperation churning inside Gillian.

Her belly clenched with unease as she surveyed the faces in the crowd. The oblivious theatergoers were practicing courtly manners and bantering among themselves, unaware of the danger around them. Somewhere within, Fouché's men were hiding in plain sight, and Gillian would have to be particularly careful not to draw any attention to herself before she met with Percival Avery, Marquess Stanton. He was a dear friend who'd worked with them on various missions, a man of many disguises who often hid behind a foppish mask. She'd contacted him immediately after Lucien's death, urgently requesting he join her in Box Three.

Stanton's access to Lord Danbury had proven beneficial to Gillian and Lucien. The two men had been fast friends, and in exchange for receiving covert training, the marquess had sworn to keep Gillian's secret, to never reveal her true occupation.

Suddenly, she gasped. *There! In the corner!*

A man stood with his back to her, but his nut-brown hair carried a familiar wave. She retreated behind a tall gentleman and waited, refusing to breathe. Her quarry turned, revealing shifty eyes, a hooked nose, and a pockmarked face.

Definitely not Simon.

Gillian took a deep breath and tried to settle her nerves before turning her attention to the staircase that led to the boxes above the Royal Box as the pulsing throng progressed toward the theater doors. To her memory, Box Three offered an excellent view of the theater. There, she'd inform Stanton about the threat to Lord Nelson's life and they could survey the space for the vice-admiral's assassin.

A feminine voice purred to her left, and Gillian chanced a look, noting that the woman's tiny, pale figure was no comparison to her own: she towered over the young miss by half.

"Do you think he'll wear his uniform, Your Grace?" the woman asked, angling her face to the light. "I hear he casts a spectacular figure, even without an arm."

A smartly fashioned duke leaned closer to the woman. "He's never without his uniform, I hear," he whispered. "And though the romantic in you would find an eye patch thrilling, Nelson does not wear one to cover his blind eye."

Gillian slipped past, making sure to keep the wall at her back and the expectant audience between her and the auditorium as she moved toward the stairs.

"He's back in England because he's ill again," another patron ventured to guess. "Malaria again, the poor fellow."

The comment was followed by a strong rebuking feminine shriek. "I don't care what the admiral has endured. He's a connoisseur of the dollies and has made himself ridiculous being seen with *that* woman. If he brings her, I shall not hold my tongue."

"Do you believe it possible for her to accompany him?" another man asked, eliciting several guffaws.

Gillian pressed her hand to her throat. She didn't know who had uttered the sarcastic remark, but it brought a half smile to her face even as her heart drummed erratically against her ribs.

"Did you say he might bring Lady Hamilton?" a feather-clad woman asked, jumping into the conversation. "I had so hoped to see Lady Nelson on his arm."

Fear gripped Gillian. Lady Nelson and Lady Hamilton were the least of the *ton's* worries. As one of a few privy to the real reason for Nelson's return, she knew that he'd been ordered to protect England's shores. The vice-admiral intended to do just that by forming a clandestine group of rogues that would be called Nelson's Tea. The organization of those mercenaries was the reason Fouché and his gendarmes—Napoleon's secret police—had put a bounty on Nelson's head.

She swallowed to moisten her dry mouth and listened more closely.

"Quite. It's all the banter on the benches," a stodgy gentleman with a nasal voice answered.

Gabble-grinders were rampant tonight. Vice-Admiral Nelson wasn't to be pitied and mocked. Instead, he should be held in the highest regard for his successful *ruse de guerre* at the Battle of Copenhagen and the peace agreement he'd secured with the Danes.

Disgust swept through Gillian with unrelenting force. What did these fashionable fools know about sacrifice? There were weightier concerns in the world than the state of Nelson's reputation. The vice-admiral saw that import routes remained open. He provided England access to rationed goods—goods the *ton* would greatly miss if he failed. In truth, if they comprehended the danger Nelson was in, that *they* were in, they'd scramble to the exits without a backward glance.

Milksops! The lot of them!

If the missive Lucien had given her was any indication, Nelson's would-be assassins were close. And with Lady Hamilton's penchant for being the center of the vice-admiral's attention, all it would take was one strike at her to cut Nelson to the marrow. Gillian pressed her lips together, placed a hand to her neck, and inhaled a tremulous breath.

Argand lamps were raised just beyond the entryway that led to the stage, and the melodious tone of the orchestra's strings signaled that the performance was about to begin. Gillian's blood vibrated through her extremities, and her nerves intensified as the crush of bodies pressed into the theater. Conversations around her grew louder as the horde ventured to the five-shilling section, where nobility and the privileged congregated. Gentry and critics paraded to the three-shilling benches in the pit, and tradesmen flocked to the two-shilling seats. Servants and *ordinary* citizens sought the one-shilling seats in the upper gallery, an extravagance they could rarely afford to pay and one that forced them to enter the theater from a separate door. It was the perfect way for assassins to sneak inside.

Her senses on high alert, Gillian wove past gentlemen, military officers, soldiers, dandies, and ladies of every persuasion, whose primary goal was to see and be seen. To mock, not be mocked, beneath the silent speculation of painted cherubs staring down from an ornate ceiling. Fortuitously, the entire theater was her stage, and everyone in it an unsuspecting player.

Five years had passed since Gillian had returned to London. The *ton* still blazed proudly like a well-oiled lamp in a murky fog—a bristling, unsettling revelation when she hadn't yearned for Society or pined for it in her absence. She'd stayed away from London, from Lord Danbury. She'd kept her sanity intact by suppressing her feelings for the man who hadn't returned her love. Now, by coming back here, she risked a confrontation with him. Would the walls she'd erected around her heart withstand such a reunion? Not in her current fragile state of mind . . .

A knot tightened in her belly. The weight of her deception, the risk to Vice-Admiral Nelson, to Lucien's memory, threatened to crush her. She struggled to catch her breath and regain control as the crowd stopped moving, blocking her escape.

Gather your courage. This isn't your first foray into dangerous waters.

No. For reasons beyond her control, she once more breathed the stench of debauchery that had been the center of her life several years earlier. She'd kept her distance until now—until her dutiful, albeit secretive and resourceful, husband's death.

Oh, how she missed Lucien. He'd been her closest friend, and although their love had not been one of romance, she didn't regret a single moment of their life together. He had taken her ideals and broadened them substantially. He'd been her hero, a staunch believer in every man's right to free will.

Beat the enemy first, negotiate afterward, Nelson had once said. These weren't the words a bereaved woman normally clung to, but then, she wasn't a normal woman.

The crowd parted, revealing a space on the staircase. Gillian hiked up the hem of her black bombazine gown and moved forward. It wouldn't be long until she was safe within Box Three, free to pass Lucien's missive to the marquess. Suddenly, her hair stood on end. An odd, disturbing shiver swept over her—familiar, yet life altering. She peered over her shoulder and spied the face of the one man she'd hoped not to see: Lord Simon Danbury.

Her heart hitched, and her breath caught. It took every ounce of her strength to remain calm and not to turn and run as if she'd been stung by a thousand bees. Mindful that she was under close scrutiny, she began to ascend the stairs without drawing attention to herself. With so much at stake, now wasn't the time to allow her past, no matter how hurtful it had been, to interfere with what she'd come to do.

"Ladies and gentlemen," a stagehand announced.

The pressing crowd came to a stop, barring her advance up the stairs. Gillian took advantage of the impediment to her passage, taking cover behind taller men to regard the motionless crowd and perhaps set her fears to rest. Had Simon seen her? Would he pursue her?

Light flickered off the papered walls beneath the candelabras, and rich hues of crimson and gold provided an opulent escape from the leaden sky outdoors. But there was no time to admire such luxuries.

Movement to her right and left belowstairs drew her gaze down to the lobby below. Men dressed in civilian garb ignored the announcer's speech, behaving noticeably different from the other theatergoers. Instead of paying rapt attention, the men assumed predatory positions at various intervals in the lobby, taking great pains to look normal as they glanced at pocket watches or read the cast list. Royal guards. Since a prior assassination attempt on King George III—one Lucien helped to circumvent—a strategic plan had been put into place to thwart any further threats to the king and his son, the Prince of Wales. Gillian had counted on these guards being present, but tonight, the threat wasn't against the king. It was against Vice-Admiral Nelson.

"The play is about to begin," the announcer continued. "Everyone take your seats!"

Another man stepped into the light. He was tall and lean

with slightly wavy, nut-brown hair that had grayed slightly at his temples. His distrusting eyes skimmed over the crowd, and he flicked his gaze to the exit and then toward her.

Filled with foreboding, Gillian shrank back behind several men. She clenched the folds of her skirts as her nerve endings throbbed to life. Beneath the scintillating, surging opera house music Lord Danbury's given name—Simon—nearly escaped her lips. Even though he stood below her, he may as well have been standing right in front of her. He was close, closer than she wanted him to be.

Concentrate!

It was hard to do when her senses reeled the way they did, however. Simon had no idea that Lucien had trained her to be his equal. He would have argued against putting Gillian in harm's way, but he'd given up that right when he'd enticed her to marry Lucien, insisting that the marriage would protect her from Drury Lane's scurrilous rakes, as well as Gillian's own abusive father, who was now deceased.

No matter what could be said of their mutual parting, Simon's ability to affect her body and soul was the only reason she hadn't wanted to fulfill Lucien's request to come to London. What she and Simon had shared was in the past, and she wanted to keep it that way. But a small sadistic part of her had known Simon would be at tonight's performance, especially with Nelson in attendance. Their friendship dated back to the vice-admiral's command of HMS *Agamemnon* and their mutual interest in protecting the king and anything, or anyone, of importance to His Majesty.

"Enjoy tonight's performance," the announcer proclaimed.

The crowd set into motion once more, successfully blocking Simon from view, and allowing her to focus on her objective. Gillian tried to ignore the anxiety coiling in her belly. She shook her head to clear it as she ascended the next level of stairs to the third floor and headed toward Box Three. Would the marquess already be waiting for her there?

The missive Lucien had given her had come from Philippe d'Auvergne, a fellow Chouan and Vice-Admiral of the Red, adopted son of Godefroy de La Tour d'Auvergne, the Duke of Bouillon. He was also a former colleague of Nelson's who operated safe houses and landing sites, and secured safe passage across the Channel Islands, smuggling people and *assignat*—counterfeit bank notes—into France to inflate its economy. From the massive tower he'd built at La Hougue Bie in Jersey, known as the Prince's Tower, d'Auvergne had discovered a plot to kill Nelson. And with the announcement of Holcroft's *Deaf and Dumb*, Gillian didn't have much time. Nelson was the Admiralty's greatest weapon. The loss of his life would jeopardize the entire future of England's fleet.

Blood thundered in her veins, the sound vibrating like drums between her ears. She had met with the marquess six months prior for another mission, but it had been years since she'd last seen Simon. Even still, the words he'd spoken to her then were as clear as if it had been yesterday.

It's for your own good, Gillian. I cannot love you. His gray eyes had held hers, imprisoning her in regret, and still, to this day, the memory managed to cut through her. Their love had not been meant to be. The sudden ache in her heart hit her with shocking force. She'd lost Simon five years ago, and now she'd lost Lucien. She wasn't sure how much more her heart could take.

You will be better off with Lucien. And I will have the luxury of knowing that you are safe, Simon had said.

Safe? Simon had no idea the course he'd set her on.

Oh, Lucien . . . She'd die before she failed him.

For a moment, Gillian glanced down at her black-gloved fingers, recalling the dark-red warmth of Lucien's blood and the last time he'd looked into her eyes.

Applause erupted, filling the immense structure with a deafening sound. Her heart skipped a beat. *No. No. No. Has Nelson already arrived?*

Promptness wasn't one of Nelson's customs at public events. He preferred making a grand entrance to acclamations and loud huzzahs. *No,* she reasoned, casually surveying the amphitheater. The applause didn't signal Nelson's arrival, but rather, it was another indication the play was about to begin.

Gillian swallowed and tempered her wildly beating heart as she pushed through the throng. Shadows danced across the walls as flickering chandeliers dangled overhead, casting a golden hue on the wave of bodies ascending above her. She'd taken precautions, donning her widow's weeds to conceal her identity—though she was a widow in a very real sense now. For Lucien, England, Nelson, and everyone seated in the opera house, she would justly sacrifice herself here and now if she could fulfill her promise to her late husband and save Nelson's life. But would she be able to?

Gillian took a deep breath and crossed herself discreetly. *So help me God.*

Two

*"They have their exits and their entrances,
And one man in his time plays many parts—"*
~William Shakespeare, As You Like It

LORD SIMON DANBURY shut out the rumors he'd heard about Vice-Admiral Horatio Nelson from the prattle-boxes before him and searched for anyone or anything suspicious in the congested foyer. Experience had taught him to be diligent, no matter the venue or how innocent people may seem. He recalled all too easily how James Hadfield had stood in the audience and taken a shot at King George III as the monarch had entered the Royal Box with the queen and princesses at his side, and the orchestra began playing "God Save the King." If not for Lucien Corbet, Baron Chauncey's assistance, the narrow miss might have cost England more than a king who'd reigned for over forty years. Deranged and determined men would do anything to further their cause, as he could attest. He worked with the former war secretary and Admiralty treasurer, Henry Dundas, to rout the United Irishmen and merchants who joined the Corresponding Societies in London, Manchester, and Yorkshire. The groups fought against the Acts of Union unifying Great Britain and Ireland, and had already plotted to kill the king and murder the Privy Council, caring nothing for King George's legacy, especially after he'd lost the Colonies.

This day, in particular, Simon had cause for worry. A hero would be in their midst. Vice-Admiral Nelson was scheduled to make an appearance after securing a hard-won peace agreement with the Danes. His arrival provided a perfect opportunity for chaos in the cultural divide. To offset trouble, strategies had been crafted to counter any attack that might take place. Citizens had swarmed to Drury Lane for a spectacle, a chance to see England's savior and offer praise in the presence of the king's son, the Prince of Wales. Anything could go wrong. And Simon would be ready to staunch any attempt to do so.

Orson, one of the hired men in Simon's employ, came to stand beside him.

"Is everyone in place?" Simon asked.

"Yes," Orson answered. "We are ready, my lord."

A streak of black caught Simon's eye. There, on the staircase landing, a widow was moving in and out of the crowd. Her veil concealed her features as she kept to several tall Corinthians' backs. And yet, her movements were not regal or sorrowful but hurried, calculated, purposefully obscuring her from view in a sea of people who yearned to see and be seen. But that wasn't all. There was something familiar about her, regardless that her widow's weeds armed his suspicions. Black wasn't fashionable in a sea of white-robed females, and mourning women usually avoided the theater.

"Is something amiss, my lord?" Orson asked.

Simon shook himself and met Orson's gaze. "No." Perhaps he was getting too old for this. "I thought I saw someone I know." To his recollection, only one woman held the kind of power over him that this one seemed to wield, only one woman moved the way she did—with purpose and as if she knew the theater like the back of her hand—a woman likely never to be purged from his soul: Gillian Stillman Corbet,

Baroness Chauncey.

Orson nodded and bowed his head. "Then if everything is in order, my lord, I will go back to my post."

"Yes." The muscles in Simon's jaw tightened. It was futile to allow the past to conflict with his duty. "You do that, Orson." He drew his head back stiffly as Orson walked to the lobby entrance then scrutinized the stairs once more. There, he caught sight of the woman again. She ducked behind another patron. Caught between elation and surprise, Simon froze, his body reacting exactly as it did whenever he saw her in his dreams.

It *was* Gillian.

Why was she here? Simon hadn't seen the woman since she'd walked away from him and out of his life forever. But he didn't believe in coincidences. He prided himself on evaluating reality with sound judgment, giving nothing away and holding nothing back. Facts were reliable; happenstance was cause for suspicion. And yet the possibility of Gillian returning to Drury Lane for the first time in five years gutted him, stealing his breath and taking him back in time to the moment he'd fought so hard to forget—the day she'd discovered he was betrothed to another.

Lucifer take it! He didn't want to feel the emotions Gillian pumped into his unwilling body.

His fingers twitched, then tightened around the silver dragon's head handle of his cane. Bollocks! He'd thought that after arranging for Gillian to marry Chauncey, he'd put her behind him. He'd resigned himself to a loveless marriage and procuring the heir his father had demanded, and Simon had relegated himself to focusing on the task at hand, living—if one could call it that—and sacrificing every ounce of his strength for the greater good. He'd done a decent job of it so far, barring his wife Edwina's debilitating illness. Now, seeing

Gillian again made him realize he'd been wrong that night so many years ago; she made him see how incomplete his marriage of convenience had become.

Why? Why are you being so stubborn? her voice pleaded faintly in the distance of his memories.

Because he was an arse.

No. No. No, you fool. It will do no good to remember.

But it was no use. The floodgates had already opened. He could no sooner fight the images of Gillian clinging to his gloved hands, her heartbreak mirroring his own as tears tumbled down her rosy cheeks, than prevent Lucien from taking her away from him forever.

Stubborn? Simon had asked her. *I should ask you the same question.*

I am only stubborn in one regard—you, she'd professed.

Her searching eyes had imprisoned his. *You are young,* he'd explained. *My hands are tied. You must turn your attentions to someone who can reciprocate your love.*

Reciprocate? I love you, Simon. I am not a child who can change the way I feel in an instant.

You must not love me, he'd told her.

Those five words cut into him for the millionth time.

We will be each other's ruin, Gillian. You know this as well as I do.

Deny your feelings all you want, but I never will, Simon. No matter how far you send me away, no matter—

Don't speak. He'd touched her mouth to end her confession before it killed him. *Go. Live. Be happy.*

He'd turned to Chauncey then, fighting the urge to rip the man apart as he came forward to grab Gillian by her elbow and lead her away to the church in Chelsea and the vows that would separate Simon from her forever. Nothing had wounded him more deeply than sending the woman he had loved to another man's bed. But an agreement had been made between the Landon-Fitzhugh family and his father, one meant to "improve Simon's naval status," one that couldn't be breached without causing a scandal of epic proportions.

Simon had told himself that if he couldn't spend his life with Gillian, he'd entrust her to his good friend and fellow spy, a French expatriate and newly appointed baron, a man who could offer respectability, marriage, and a life free of suspicion and disdain that a career at Drury Lane could not.

Blast his damnable pride and his inability to refuse his father's demands! None of what he'd done had been worth the damage to his soul, or to Edwina's.

Simon leaned on his cane for balance. He was a hedonistic man, a cad for having loved another man's wife when his own was lying bedridden, a fact that damned Simon to eternity. He and Edwina shared respect, friendship, and companionship, it was true, but never the deep, abiding love he'd known with Gillian. Even time seemed to wage war against him.

"Listen, my lord," a soft-spoken woman said excitedly to her companion, "the play is about to begin."

The lady's escort curtly said, "Perhaps that will prod this throng to move."

Sounds of the orchestra and the casual banter continued as Simon inhaled a stabilizing breath and regarded the stairs. There, like a goddess who had assumed human flesh, the lovely widow ascended the staircase before him. She was Baroness Chauncey; there was no doubt.

But how could it be?

Simon grumbled to himself. Chauncey had once mentioned a widow he'd enlisted to help him on his endeavors. Could that grief-stricken woman have actually been Gillian? She was an experienced actress, after all . . .

No, it wasn't possible. Gillian couldn't be a spy. He'd know if she was. Wouldn't he?

Bloody hell! The baroness was not the kind of distraction he needed this night. The Prince of Wales was in the Royal Box, and Nelson would be arriving soon. Still, he was instinctively focused on Gillian. Whatever her ruse—destitute widow needing solace, or spy dressed to kill—her suspicious actions clamored for his attention.

Determined to find out what was going on, Simon lifted the handle of his cane slightly and suppressed a satisfied grin as the sound of scraping steel pierced the air. Then he quickly slid his blade back inside its secretive sheath. He gave the weapon a sideways glance before redirecting his gaze to Gillian's fading bombazine skirts. Since arriving at the theater, he'd anticipated a quiet night of boring society mixed with an aura of intrigue. Gillian's appearance at Drury Lane had awakened his senses to a heated chase, one he'd desperately longed for to ease his boredom. He bit down on another smile as he walked forward.

At thirty-three, Simon was a man in his prime and was used to long hours and taking to his regrettably cold bed without sating his baser needs. He and Edwina lived separate lives: she taking solace in medicinal remedies, and he fighting for something larger than himself. He loathed gentlemen who were unwilling to serve the greater good. And he was determined not to fail the Prince of Wales or Vice-Admiral Nelson.

Perhaps Simon was wrong. Perhaps the widow wasn't Gillian. He prayed he was mistaken, but he was hardly ever wrong.

"Have you noticed that widow, my lord?" his smartly dressed head of security, John Cavendish, asked abruptly on his left. "It is rare to see one at the theater."

The man was confirming Simon's suspicions. Wearing black in general served a useful purpose—disguise—but it certainly wasn't proper for this setting.

Simon stopped to survey the crowd. "Yes," he finally answered. "Leave her to me. Until I return, see to it that no one gets near Lord Nelson when he arrives."

Cavendish's brow furrowed. "Are you leaving?"

"No." The question was ridiculous. He never left a job unfinished. "I shall return momentarily after I question the widow. Until then, keep a vigilant eye on the entrance to the theater. Leave nothing to chance. I want everything still in order when the admiral appears. We have no way of knowing if the audience will swarm him."

"Yes, my lord." Cavendish bowed, then spun around briskly, revealing his military training.

Curse the man for neglecting to hide that small, critical detail. The idea was to remain inconspicuous!

Rule number one: A man had to always be on guard. In war, at peace, and at the gaming tables, one should never give away a tell unless absolutely necessary.

Simon limped toward the stairs. He quirked his brow and peered into the crushing throng, determined to only briefly disrupt his usual duties to discover what she was up to.

Then Simon frowned. If the baroness was there, Chauncey couldn't be far behind, which would mean . . .

Was there another threat against the king? The only time Chauncey had ever been to the Theatre Royal had been to thwart an assassination attempt on King George. Besides which, the baron's last message indicated he'd smuggled himself into France on a mission of great importance. If Chauncey had returned to London without making Simon aware, it was a circumstance that didn't allow for the baroness to leave Drury Lane before any information the baron had attained in France was in Simon's hands.

But no, that couldn't be the case. Because if Simon prided himself on anything, it was his vast knowledge about England's foreign policy. He was kept informed of everything there was to know, thanks to his former role as a Royal Navy officer. At the Prince of Wales's insistence, he'd gleaned a network of intelligence for the Admiralty, an association that included diplomatic ties to Vice-Admiral Nelson and Henry Dundas.

Had crucial intelligence truly been kept from him?

Simon meandered through the crowd and ascended the stairs with the aid of his cane, desiring more than ever to lift the mysterious veil from Gillian's face. Black fabric, ribbons, and lace obscured the subtle upward turn of her nose. She moved like a prowling alley cat, one he knew could wield a diplomat's wit.

Simon bristled. If any credence could be given to the renewed vigor flowing through his limbs, it was this. He had an unyielding connection to the baroness that had not died as much as he'd tried to kill it.

A storm of bitter frustration brewed within him as he watched her cautiously regard her surroundings before disappearing into a private box on the third level. He'd made it his own personal mission to know every inch of the Theatre Royal, and it so happened that the particular owner of the box she'd chosen, the Duke of Bedford, was grieving the untimely death of his wife, Duchess Bedford. The only way for her to enter the box would have been to rent it from Bedford himself or to know the particulars of the duke's misfortune.

In good conscience, he couldn't walk away without knowing whether or not his mind had jumped to conclusions. He had to know what Gillian was up to and that she, the Prince of Wales, and Nelson were safe. Determination fueling him, Simon hurried up to the third level, pulled back the curtains to Bedford's box, and stepped inside.

His heart—the damned thumping organ—threatened to burst from his chest as his eyes adjusted to the bright lights shimmering from the stage, charging the box's darkness with overpowering energy. Gillian stood erect, her shoulders firmly set, alerting him that she knew someone was there. It took every ounce of his strength not to rush to her and pull her close in full view of the audience.

"I knew it was only a matter of time before you found me," she said. "Still, I had hoped to fool you—of all people—the most."

He was jolted by her comment, and a deafening pulse pounded in his ears. "We are too alike, you and I." He stepped closer, anxiously removing his gloves, needing something to do, but he was tempted beyond reason to lay his hand on her shoulder and turn her around to face him.

Fool!

He wasn't a nervous man. Eager, yes, but he'd never been anxious around a woman, until her.

"Why are you purposefully trying to avoid me?" he asked.

"You forget, I do not have to answer to you, my lord," she replied with admirable severity.

Her reminder cut deep, more thoroughly than the old wound on his side. "You are out of humor with me. I don't blame you for wishing me to perdition." He removed his hat, irritated that his affections for her could be so easily rekindled. He brushed his hair back away from his face.

What she must think of him?

He cleared his throat. "I had hoped that time would heal your wounds."

"Some injuries never heal."

How true that statement was . . .

It was all he could do to keep space between them. How foolish of him to desire her still. Aghast, he tightened his grip on his top hat to keep from acting upon the inclination to do anything untoward, even though every inch of him shouted at him to take her into his arms. He thought he'd never see her again.

Hypocrite! Bloody fool! You cannot relive the past.

"Let us not quarrel, Baroness," he said. "Pray, please forgive my offense. I never meant to hurt you."

She lifted her head enough for him to notice. "Time has changed us both, my lord. I hold no grudge against you. You must forgive yourself, for I am—I have been—happy."

He nodded. "I am glad of it." Her brutal honesty tore through him, somehow managing to ease his discomfort slightly. While he wanted to tell Gillian that he'd never stopped loving her, too many obstacles stood between them.

Had she chosen her pretense of mourning to honor the Duchess of Bedford's passing? Would that not draw attention to Bedford's box all the more? The theater was host to curious onlookers with opera glasses who spied on the audience and studied the boxes with care, searching for glimpses of scandal that would last throughout the coming months.

Still, he stood like a lost lamb in the silence that stretched between them and waited for Gillian to speak.

She lifted her small, delicate, gloved hands and pushed back her veil, revealing startlingly fair skin and the generous lips that haunted his dreams, making his heartbeat quicken. Her dark brown gaze slowly met his as she turned. The dull light reflecting in her eyes revealed she *had* changed—exponentially so. And her precise movements, timed almost too perfectly, unnerved him.

"I thought . . . if I ever laid eyes on you again, I'd cease to exist," she said.

He was thankful she hadn't fainted dead away as she was too close to the edge of the box. "And yet here you are, standing and breathing." He stepped toward her, hoping to coax her away from the handrail. "You give yourself little credit—"

"No." She held her hand up between them. "Don't come any closer."

He'd gone too far—again. *Damn!* What was it about this particular woman that unhinged him so? "You are still the most beautiful woman I've ever seen," he admitted. "Country life agrees with you."

She nodded. Her black hair was parted down the middle and swept back neatly behind her ears. Her heart-shaped face led his eyes directly to her intelligent brows, pert nose, and the very same rose-tinged, bow-shaped mouth that had once proclaimed her love for him. To further accentuate her delicate, aristocratic looks, pearl earrings dangled from her earlobes, drawing his attention agonizingly lower to the nape of her neck, which was partially concealed by a black fichu.

"The credit, Lord Danbury, goes to my husband."

Her words gutted him afresh. "Of course," he said, thoroughly chastised. He cleared his throat. "Where is the baron? I half expect him to suddenly accost me from the shadows."

Gillian's expression sobered. "I left him in the country." Her chin quivered strangely, and her brows arched almost imperceptibly.

Simon narrowed his eyes. The baron would never allow Gillian to travel to London without him. Something was wrong. He felt it in his bones, sensed it with an uncanny, crippling awareness.

"Gillian," he said, reaching for her hand.

She snatched her fingers back as if stung. "Baroness, my lord."

"I know who you are and from whence you come." Damned if her marriage to Chauncey wasn't etched into his brain. "I'm the last man on earth who needs to be reminded."

Her expression hardened. "Perhaps not."

"Why are you here?" he finally asked. Taking a deep breath to regain control, Simon swallowed back his amazement at how quickly his desire for a woman he couldn't have had risen to the surface. It was a rush of passion so brutal and all-consuming, he could barely withstand it.

She didn't answer.

A gamut of conflicting emotions assailed him. "Why are you here, Baroness?" he asked again, abiding by her wishes. "Has something happened?"

Gillian stepped backward and peered down at the assembling crowd, as if searching for someone in particular. If not for Chauncey, then for whom?

"'Tis no concern of yours . . . for now," she confided. Her voice held an undecipherable edge. What did she know? What had occurred that made her come back to London? To Simon's knowledge, she'd sequestered herself in Kent for the past five years. She wouldn't return unless there was justification to do so.

He was determined not to be put off. "You once swore you'd never return to the theater, and you are dressed in widow's weeds . . . Why?"

"For reasons I cannot explain at this moment. Now, if you don't mind, I have been long without culture, and Holcroft's *Deaf and Dumb* is about to begin." She smiled coquettishly, once more dismissing him.

"I'm disinclined to believe that is the only reason you are here."

She forced another smile. "You may presume whatever you like. What you believe is none of my concern."

"It should be," he said firmly.

Her eyes narrowed into slits. The air around them charged like brilliant light crisscrossing a fused sky. Oh, how she must hate him.

He made every effort to remain calm, to prevent her from seeing how deeply wounded he was by her insolence. "When have you ever seen a widow at the opera? If you intended not to draw attention to yourself, you have failed. Black attire is an unusual choice. It leads me to recall one particular time your masquerading as a widow earned a disagreeable end . . ."

"How dare you remind me of Sarah Siddons," she said, her tone carefully controlled. "I worked extremely hard to portray Lady Macbeth. If not for my father . . ." Gillian turned away from him. "I cannot go on. Leave," she whispered. "Before it's too late."

"Too late?" He huffed. "What has taken hold of you? It's unlike you to be so nervous."

"I am not nervous. I am all anticipation," she said. Her words wavered slightly as she stepped farther into the shadows. "It has been too long since . . . I've attended a production." She stared strangely at her hands, making him wonder what was fascinating her. She glanced up, her eyes sullen, transformed. Was it because she still hated him?

"Time has never been on our side, Simon."

Lucifer take it, she'd finally used his given name. A disemboweling dagger couldn't have done more damage. If he didn't do something soon, he was going to bleed out. And that simply would not do. "Gillian," he said, unable to control the passion that crept into his voice. "Something is wrong. I can feel it. I assure you, I can give you—"

"Nothing," she said with split-second timing. She turned back to look at him, a forlorn smile on her face. "This is something I must do."

Did she hate him that much?

"You aren't going to tell me why you are here, are you?"

Three

*"His acts being seven ages. At first, the infant . . .
Mewling and puking in the nurse's arms."*
~*William Shakespeare,* As You Like It

Lucien's death was a raw wound, but Gillian did not feel it the way a lover would. She had little guilt about not having consummated her vows. Their marriage agreement had been more binding than any spiritual coupling, and yet, it was so unlike the way she was drawn to Simon. She despised how she yearned to be held by him, touched by him, kissed by him, never to be parted—even after all these years. Her husband had always understood who'd pulled her heartstrings. He'd used that knowledge to empower her, train her, mold her into an equal partner, so that one day, when the time was right, she would have all the opportunities in the world.

"You have no hold over me, Simon." With an upward tilt of her chin, she presented a brave face, pressing home the fact that he could try to make her tell him why she was at Drury Lane but that she'd never relent. She didn't have to. She'd grown stronger of character because of Lucien, and perhaps more stubborn, if that was possible. "I am perfectly capable of taking care of myself."

Was she? The product of a penniless father who prized ale

over blood, she'd been performing in the theater when she'd first met Simon, alongside notable greats like Elizabeth Farren, Frances Abington, and siblings Sarah Siddons and John Philip Kemble. Siddons had a habit of bedding patrons. And amid the realization that Simon was fated to marry another, Gillian had not been above destroying her own reputation to become Simon's bird of paradise. What a fool she'd been then. No longer.

A knot rose in her throat, making it exceptionally hard to swallow.

"I know you *believe* you can take care of yourself," Simon said. "But I assigned you a protector, Gillian, someone to keep you safe from men who targeted actresses, men like your father, and yet, you are here, dressed like a character from one of your plays. Now, please, tell me the truth. Where is the baron?" Simon stepped ever closer. "I know he met with d'Auvergne in Jersey. Hasn't he returned from France? Is something amiss? Why are you alone?"

"You should go," she said softly, refusing to answer his questions. "Go."

AGAIN, SIMON WAS met by a defiant mix of stubbornness and sorrow. Then mind-boggling silence. Disgruntled but spurred to action, Simon slapped his hat on his head and began to shove on his gloves. *A gentleman wouldn't have removed his gloves at all,* he berated himself. *But I am no gentleman.* Gentlemen didn't fixate on married women. And *married* gentlemen didn't betray infirm wives, no matter the arrangement.

Oh, his sins were many—too many to count. Damn his eyes! On entering Bedford's box, a small part of him had held out hope that Gillian still loved him. But he'd chosen his path, and in doing so, he'd lost Gillian forever. Lies and misery separated them now. Hers. His. Bloody hell, they'd never been fated to be together, and nothing he could do or say would change that.

Gillian, Baroness Chauncey had become resourceful, cunning, and ruthless in her dealings with him. He deserved every cutting remark, every heated look. But that would not stop him from discovering the reason for her presence in Town. He'd get to the bottom of it, with or without her help.

Regret rose like a deafening buffer between them as applause ignited the crowd below and in the boxes around them. Lighting in the theater had dimmed. The play had begun. And Nelson was late, as usual, which meant Simon needed to return to his duties.

"Promise me you will not leave until our conversation is finished," he said as he made his way to the curtained exit.

"I cannot." She slanted a look at him. "I will not."

His brows shot up in surprise. "As you wish, but I will be back."

Holcroft's *Deaf and Dumb* began like the metaphor it was—neither character understanding the other, neither ready to accept their true feelings, neither willing to make more sacrifices than had already been made. Gillian stood before him, proud and undaunted with her chin raised and eyes set with unflinching determination.

Simon bowed, barely catching her polite curtsey. "Baroness," he said stiffly before sweeping the curtain to the side.

She made no sound.

Perhaps it is for the best, eh? his conscience prodded.

Duty linked him to Vice-Admiral Nelson, to a cause greater than flesh. The mission they embarked on together—he and Nelson—organizing a group of mercenaries that would answer to the vice-admiral and act to stop Napoleon's threat of invasion, depended on total discretion and his complete concentration. As quickly as his instincts had been triggered to follow Gillian, Simon forced her to the back of his mind, turning off his emotions as he exited the box. His heart was not equipped for the gut-wrenching truth that Gillian wanted nothing to do with him. So be it. A man could not turn back the tide.

Simon tapped his cane on the floor of the corridor. Not far from the stairs, a tall gentleman dressed in brilliant gold, powdered hair and face—it was ghastly old-fashioned for so young a person—caught his attention. The foppish marquess obliterated any sense of normalcy from the modern mind, which was exactly what the young fellow wanted. Simon rolled his eyes. Percival Avery, the Marquess of Stanton pushed the limits of disguise as far as any man could and still managed to maintain surprising dignity. How did the man do it?

"Od's fish, Danbury," the popinjay called, waving his quizzing glass like a drunken sailor with a bottle of rum. He sauntered closer on loose legs that gave him a swaggering, jaunty gait. "Have you seen a woman in black swishing her bombazine skirts on this level?" He bowed respectfully.

Simon's brow rose as he bowed in return. Bloody hell, how was he supposed to forget about Gillian if Stanton, in all his outlandish finery, intended to seek her out? He could not forget the man was not a dandy in the real sense but a rake through and through. The irony? The marquess was the son of Rathbone Avery, the fourth Duke of Blendingham, who was a prominent member of the House of Lords. With an aristocratic heritage dating back hundreds of years, Stanton was in the upper echelon of society, the perfect position for a man of means to discern secrets, foil devious pursuits, and champion king and country without anyone being the wiser.

It had been Stanton's idea to perform the dandy to perfection, much to the consternation of his father. He'd fashioned his look after Georgian lords and French kings, even applying a beauty mark aptly positioned on his cheek near the side of his nose. Trained by Chauncey and in line to inherit a seat in the House of Lords, Stanton was one of Simon's best agents, a firstborn son willing to protect the Crown while performing machinations of status and wealth.

"Marquess," Simon said with a bow, maintaining his distance so no one would be the wiser about their association. "What business would a man like you have with that chit?"

"Egad!" the marquess exclaimed. "Are you implying something positively scandalous, dear fellow? Because if you are, I'm on board." He winked.

Jealousy raged within Simon at the thought of Stanton and Gillian alone in Box Three. "You and a mysterious woman—"

"Aha!" Stanton exclaimed, pointing his quizzing glass. "You—"

"Are tantamount to trouble," Simon finished.

"Folly is a man's best friend." The marquess cocked his brow and winked, slanting his gaze to a woman who passed by on the arm of a young man before singling out Simon again. "Do tell."

Stanton didn't have an indelicate bone in his body. In reality, the man was eight years Simon's junior, a rogue of shocking means, and a methodical man with a penchant for protecting those unable to protect themselves. This meant if Gillian needed assistance she was in capable hands. And yet her distrust of Simon himself stung.

"As John Wesley said, 'Catch on fire with enthusiasm and people will come for miles to watch you burn,'" Stanton said, dropping a hint at his purpose.

The mention of fire inside the Theatre Royal, packed as it was, sent a chill down Simon's spine. "And is the collective enthusiasm combustible?" he asked, a frisson of concern boring through him.

"Brilliant." Stanton fanned himself with an effeminate wave, then picked a gilded snuffbox out of his waistcoat, opened the lid, fingered a pinch, and delicately sniffed the tobacco into each nostril.

Get on with it, man!

"I just received my token to the inferno."

"I have received no such token," he said, tempering his frustration.

"Ah, that *is* rather revealing, isn't it?" Stanton knew about Simon and Gillian's past. He supposed the comment was meant to dig at his pride. "La, there could be a need for at least a score more to be urgently distributed about. I wouldn't dally in your pursuit."

"I see." Simon understood Stanton's code. They'd worked on it together for many years in other clandestine missions together. Now they were in league with Nelson and Dundas as Simon put together an extraordinary group of first sons from every walk of life, eager to serve England in any capacity—a group they planned to call Nelson's Tea, aptly named for the vice-admiral's penchant for the beverage. Many prospective agents longed for a steady income or the thrill of the hunt; others sought a quick rise in military rank, a political engine known for its agonizing delays. This was the main reason Nelson had come to London—other than speaking in the House of Lords and attending tonight's performance. "What kind of token do you have?" he asked.

"I can only speculate, you see," Stanton said, "because the weight of my coin is safely harbored here." He pointed to his heart.

The fire referred to danger, as related to the previous year's attempt on the king's life. The coin, a sovereign, was a token, harbored in Stanton's heart.

Christ! He was talking about Vice-Admiral Nelson!

39

Stanton leaned closer and whispered, "Fire will likely erupt this night—" He cut himself off as two men with suspiciously shifty eyes drew near. It was obvious the marquess didn't want them to overhear their conversation. "If I do not find the skirt I seek . . ." Stanton raised his quizzing glass and shifted his attention to Simon's cravat, tapping the fabric garnished with an emerald pin. "Been to Weston's, I see. Capital."

"Indeed." Simon opened his mouth to speak but held his tongue, playing along. "If you'll excuse me, Marquess, I will not delay you any further." He straightened his cuffs as the two unknown men wearing tan beaver hats nodded and entered Box Four.

"Keep your eyes on those two. Wolves in sheep's clothing. Frenchies by the look of them." Stanton's brow crooked, and his gaze followed the men until they disappeared.

Simon felt the blood drain from his face. "Of course."

"Have faith," the marquess said, instantly shifting course. "A man should not be in a hurry unless the building he's in is burning down." He made as if to leave, then turned back to Simon. "Oh, and remember: spare nothing when it comes to fashion, my good man." He spun his quizzing glass around deftly and settled it in his waistcoat. "One's attire has more power than rhetoric."

Which truly meant he should keep what is in his jacket—his weapon—close.

"Of course," Simon said, nodding.

Stanton bowed his head, then straightened. "Remember, dear sir," he said more loudly, tapping his apparel, "you will never look the aristocrat without a crisply tied cravat."

Something about the two men had piqued Stanton's curiosity. But what? Simon had seen the men milling about downstairs and had not noticed anything out of the ordinary.

Simon snarled and shoved fashion and Box Four out of

his mind, concentrating on Gillian instead. The marquess had a way of wooing women and seducing information from even the most unsuspecting dolt. His tactics were legendary, which would make him an asset Nelson's Tea could not do without.

Without a farewell, Stanton sauntered off, peeking in every curtained doorway. He offered apologies to the men in Box Four, then entered Box Three. "Ah!" Simon heard him say elatedly. "There you are, good lady. Let the games begin." The marquess disappeared inside Bedford's box.

Deuce it all! What was going on?

Nothing but England matters. Remember that.

In his line of work, any other thought process got one killed. A facade was the order of the day if he wanted to save lives. And thousands of souls were in jeopardy. Every British citizen depended on the vice-admiral's plan to offset Napoleon's quest for control over the Channel and the British Isles. Joseph Fouché and Bertrand Barère de Vieuzac were united in their efforts to support Napoleon's schemes. They would not abandon the self-proclaimed emperor, which meant England was on the brink of war.

And that left him little time to deliberate over personal happiness. Not for Gillian. Not for his wife. And certainly not for himself.

Four

*"Then the whining schoolboy, with his satchel
And shining morning face, creeping like snail
Unwilling to school. And then the lover . . ."*
~William Shakespeare, As You Like It

GILLIAN SAT BESIDE Percival Avery, Marquess Stanton as the curtains parted and actors began breaking into choreographed song and dance. Vice-Admiral Nelson had not yet made his grand entrance.

Stanton leaned close, the intimate confines of Box Three hammering home the reminder that assassins could be collaborating anywhere in the theater. "I thought I'd never get rid of him," he admitted.

Gillian sighed. "Danbury is not the worst of our problems."

"That's what I've always loved about you, Baroness. You get to the point." He smiled, seeming riveted. "Now, how so?"

"I-I—" She choked on the words, unable to reveal the truth, to tell the marquess that Lucien was dead.

Stanton's eyes flashed strangely as if he sensed how close she was to collapse. "Do you like what Holland has done with the place?" She had no desire to debate architecture or Henry Holland's design, but she knew what the marquess was doing.

The sly fellow sought to calm her by changing the subject, and his tactic was succeeding, putting her at ease. "Personally, I prefer 'Old Drury,'" he said. "These acoustics frustrate me. I can barely hear what the actors are saying." His lips twitched as he pointed to the horseshoe-shaped boxes, the lacy hem of his sleeve dangling over his fingers. "It amazes me what the owners will sacrifice to bring in three thousand paying customers. Have you heard that Drury Lane is bigger than any other place in Europe now?"

"Stanton . . ." Gillian swallowed back tears. "I am not here to enjoy the theater."

He lowered his hand to hers and squeezed. "Perhaps a little culture would do you a bit of good. You seem—" he studied her, his expression falling "—crushed."

Unable to hold his compassionate gaze any longer, she looked away. "My decision to come to London was not based on pleasure."

"In any case," he said, continuing his attempt to distract her, "I beg you to come again when the stage is set for boating. Performing a sea battle below with actual water is quite the technological marvel. I never would have thought it possible myself, and yet, I have seen it with my own eyes." He stared at the lone portrait of a boy hanging center stage, a puzzled expression distorting his handsome, powdered features. "Is that supposed to be Darlemont's son, the mute child he left for dead on a Parisian street?"

Oh, how their lives, what they sought to accomplish, paralleled Darlemont's palace of secrets, suspicion, and deceit. They both played parts in a charade: Stanton portraying the fop to perfection when nothing could be further from the truth, and Gillian trying to finish what her husband had started. The irony wasn't lost on her, but it gave her the time she needed to compose herself.

She surveyed the crowd below. The audience was focused on the lead actress. The woman's name escaped Gillian, and she chastised herself for not paying attention to the introductions, especially when, as a former actress, she understood the importance of recognition. If she'd had the time and if she'd been on an errand of amusement, she'd have researched the playbook more thoroughly. What she did *not* miss, however, was the actress's perfectly clear singing voice, albeit seemingly distant on the massive stage.

The hair rose on the back of Gillian's neck as she searched the theater for any hint of criminal behavior. Every seat in the house was occupied, save for a few inattentive patrons milling about and refusing to wait until intermission to speculate on the particulars of the crowd. The entire setting was perfectly tuned for a malicious attack by Napoleon's gendarmes.

She bit her lip to stifle a maddening scream, feeling the walls of the box closing in. The tell must have alerted Stanton to her distress.

"Out with it." Stanton gave her hand another squeeze. "Why are you here? What is so urgent that you couldn't wait for Chauncey to return from France? You know it isn't safe for a woman to travel alone."

"I had no choice." Bile rose in the back of her throat. "The baron is . . . is dead."

Stanton's mouth gaped open. "The devil you say!" he said in a whispered rush. Muscles flexed in his jaw, and she feared his teeth would crack by the force. "It's not possible. I refuse to believe it."

"Possible . . . and sadly, true," she said, the emotions she'd tried to shutter welling to the surface. "I would never lie about such a thing."

Stanton released her hand. He cleared his throat and adjusted his cravat, as if not knowing what to do or say. "I do not—cannot—believe it." His dark eyes hooded like a hawk's. "What happened?" A faint tremor shook his voice.

Gillian raised a quivering hand to wipe an errant tear off her cheek. "Lucien never believed King George's attempted assassins had worked alone." She lowered her voice to a soft whisper, conscious of the fact that it might carry in the theater. "He suspected the new order in France was responsible and that Napoleon had turned his attention on England once more. As you know, Lucien met with Philippe d'Auvergne in Jersey, who'd stumbled upon another assassination plot, one that would destroy all of England's hopes."

"Do they plan to try to kill the king again?" His voice was thick and unsteady.

"No," she said. "Another."

Stanton leaned so close she could smell his sandalwood-and-spice scent. "Who?"

"Lucien said . . ." She fought back images of Lucien lying dead before her. "I—"

"What happened?" he asked, sober as a priest. "Who is the intended target?"

"Lucien," she continued, not answering his question, "would not be deterred, no matter the danger to himself. I'm here because of what he told me on his dying breath."

"You were there? Did they—" He took hold of her hand. "Have you been hurt?"

"No." She shook her head. "His killer did not suspect Polaris would bring me to him. I took the bastard by surprise and killed him before he could . . ." She covered her mouth with her free hand. "But I was too late, Stanton. Lucien was already mortally wounded."

Stanton's expression hardened. "What did he say?"

She dropped her hand, embarrassed at how it shook uncontrollably. "Napoleon's quest will not be complete until he has dominion over England. Fouché was at the heart of King George's assassination attempt."

Stanton leaned back in his chair. "I was there, remember? James Hadfield was convicted of the deed. We caught him red-handed. His guilt and his insanity was proven by trial. I have always agreed Bannister Truelock, that religious fanatic, drove Hadfield to believe he was bringing about the second coming of Christ by eradicating the monarchy," he said, his tone laced with sarcasm.

But there was more Stanton didn't know. "Bannister Truelock may or may not have influenced Hadfield; that point is moot now as they are both in Bedlam. D'Auvergne told Lucien that the head wounds Hadfield had received after the Battle of Tourcoing were part of a process to condition Hadfield and then return him to England to kill the king."

Stanton's dark eyes sharpened. "Did d'Auvergne provide proof of this?"

She stared at him, aghast. Lucien had died trying to deliver this message. How dare Stanton accuse her husband of leading them false!

"There is to be another attempt this very night," she said succinctly. Nothing would stop her from sharing what Lucien had told her now. She'd ridden night and day to save the Baron of the Nile's life, stopping only long enough to obtain fresh horses. "Lucien barely escaped France with his life, Stanton. When he arrived in England, he was ruthlessly attacked, surviving only long enough to confess that vital information to me. Soon after h-he . . . I fled. There was no time to bury him before Fouché's men gave chase."

Stanton grasped Gillian by the wrist. His touch was gentle, assuring, which was contrary to the way his throat bobbed as he swallowed and his eyes blazed with unbridled anger. "You did what you had to do." His expression was pained. "Now . . . did he provide you with anything specific, dates, coordinates?"

"Admiral Nelson."

"Admiral Nelson?" Stanton asked. He paused, momentarily speechless, and then cleared his throat. "Is that all he said?"

She shook her head. "Lord Nelson is the intended target." Her gaze settled on Stanton's dark eyes, stark against his powdered skin. Emotions she recognized all too well—doubt, anger, horror—flashed across his face. Lucien had paid a deadly price for this information. "According to d'Auvergne's letter, Napoleon is campaigning in Egypt and Austria but has a plan to activate the *Armée des côtes de l'Océan*. Apparently, Napoleon believes that if he can neutralize Admiral Nelson and the English fleet, his own will be unstoppable."

"That plan has been in place for at least twenty years." Stanton's body tensed, and he inhaled sharply. "Never doubt a good plan. Where will he bottleneck his fleet?"

"Italy, Belgium, and France."

"But Nelson made a mockery of Boulogne," he said.

"Things are not as they were months ago, I'm afraid."

"Well if that doesn't make me fly to the time of day!" He cast an irritated glance toward the stage, then turned back to her. "That isn't the worst of it, is it?"

"No, it's not," she said, summoning her inner strength. "I arranged to meet you here because Fouché's men plan to assassinate Admiral Nelson *tonight*."

Stanton's brow cocked at an odd angle, and his gaze narrowed on her. "Tonight?"

"Yes." She allowed herself a nostalgic smile. "My husband counted you as one of few trusted friends. He specifically sent me to you, Stanton, because he knew you could stop this if I got to you in time."

"If what you say is true, Danbury must also be told."

"Yes, of course," she agreed. "The opera has just begun, and Nelson hasn't yet arrived. You have time to warn him. My one request is that you wait to leave this box until I am gone."

Stanton grabbed both Gillian's hands. "This is not the time for theatrics." His touch, while gentler than before, allowed no escape. "No one is suggesting that you face Danbury alone, m'dear." He paused. "Lucien is gone; you need a protector now."

He was right. The gendarmes were after her, but she couldn't tell Stanton that. Vice-Admiral Nelson needed everyone to guard his back.

Her world had been torn out from under her, and she was more afraid now than she'd ever been. Lucien had given her life purpose. As a widow, certain lifestyles opened up for her—that of a dowager, governess, or courtesan, or she could even remarry—but none of it appealed. She wanted her old life back, the comfort Lucien's presence gave her and the freedom she'd been given to live in a man's world with a husband who'd educated her on weaponry and books.

Candlelight flickered on the impressive stage. "I should go," she said.

"You cannot run away." Stanton's mouth curved with tenderness, disarming her. "Chauncey wouldn't want you to."

She stared into Stanton's inquisitive eyes, eyes that hid an elusive secret she'd had a hand in masterminding. "Careful," she said. "Do not presume to tell me what I can or cannot do."

"I presume nothing. However," he said, testing the lace at the cuff of his sleeve, "I saw the look on Danbury's face after he left this box. What do you think he will do when he discovers you are responsible for over half of Chauncey's successful missions in France or that you trained me?"

She didn't want to find out. "It isn't wise to threaten me, Marquess."

"I'm well aware." He harrumphed. "If you are smart—and I know you are—you'd tell him."

"I came here to deliver Lucien's last words, nothing more. Take my message to Danbury," she said, her pride giving way to duty.

"There is no reason for alarm. I assure you," the marquess said, "Admiral Nelson is not in danger here."

"And neither was King George," she countered. "Now, there's no time to lose. You must report to Danbury all I have said."

The marquess stood and bowed with a flourish of his hand. She suspected it was to appease anyone who happened to be watching them more than to be chivalrous. "I will go, but Danbury is a stubborn man. He will insist on speaking with you again."

"Rest assured, I am in no danger now." Gillian looked straight ahead, hating the bitter taste the lie left in her mouth. If she drew attention to herself, she could divert the vice-admiral's would-be assassins until the marquess and Simon could stop them. "Saving the admiral's life is all that matters now."

"You matter, Baroness."

Stanton's declaration startled her. He lifted her veil and placed his palm against her cheek. It was an alarmingly kind gesture, but anyone who took note of it would be led to speculate as to the cause of the intimacy.

"You sacrificed everything to warn us," he said. "As Chauncey's friend, I invite you to come to my townhouse. I'll see you safely settled from this day forward." He held up his hand when she opened her mouth to disagree. "No objections. I owe it to him."

She nodded. The marquess was right, of course. But she couldn't think about that now.

Gooseflesh prickled her skin as her senses came alive. Danger lurked everywhere: in the boxes beside her where foreign words floated to her ears on infrequent musical pauses, in the boxes across from her where innumerable opera glasses perched on inquisitive noses, on the stage, and in the audience seated below.

Stanton lowered her veil and reached for her wrap. He draped it around her shivering shoulders. She accepted the cloak numbly, knowing without doubt that the chill she was experiencing wasn't from the cold but from costlier ache. Lucien was gone.

She bowed her head and gathered what little courage she had left, for she had no intention of accompanying the marquess to his townhouse. "I'll do as you say, on one condition." She smiled. "Mention nothing of my whereabouts to Lord Danbury."

Stanton nodded warily. "He'll ask."

"That isn't your concern," she said.

"But it is. You've put me in a precarious situation, Baroness."

"I am sorry for that. Truly, I am." Her chest tightened, and she was at once besieged by a sensation that she was being watched. She quickly forgot the marquess and, blinking back tears, reached for the opera glasses sitting nearby. She raised them to her eyes and studied the stage, then arrowed the lens at the boxes across from her. When nothing appeared out of the ordinary, she glanced over the audience until, almost by instinct, she was drawn to Simon. He stood with his back against the wall, a hand on his cane, and one knee bent, his agile body tilted toward the exit. Ever on guard, he was waiting on Vice-Admiral Nelson's arrival. Feeling trapped, she said, "You must go now. Warn him."

Stanton touched her shoulder. "Careful, lest you give yourself away, m'dear."

"What the devil do you mean?" she asked breathlessly, lowering the glasses and turning to look at him.

"If Fouché's men followed you here, or if they are lying in

wait to achieve devious ends, you draw attention to yourself by showing interest in the crowd. You are supposed to be a widow, remember?" His throat bobbed, as if he was strangled on his words. He took several steps backward. "Oh dear, I didn't mean—"

The lead actress stopped mid-aria. Violins screeched to a halt. The audience began to murmur, loudly turning in their seats to stare at the opening of the amphitheater.

There, in all his military splendor, was the gallant Vice-Admiral Lord Horatio Nelson. He stood in the vaulted doorway, his face animated and confident. His mistress, Lady Emma Hamilton, decorated his left arm.

Gillian swallowed. It was beginning . . .

Five

*"Sighing like furnace, with a woeful ballad
Made to his mistress' eyebrow. Then a soldier,
Full of strange oaths and bearded like the pard..."*
~William Shakespeare, As You Like It

"GOOD GOD! WE'VE taken too long. You must go," she exclaimed, turning only to discover Stanton had already left the box.

They could not fail. She'd promised Lucien she'd do everything within her power to save this great man of England. But perhaps Simon was right. She was a liar, incapable of love. She'd given up on the man she had truly loved and had married another, diligently obeying her vows, but she had not loved Lucien the way a man deserved to be loved. She'd struggled to forget Simon, and what's more, she hadn't listened to her instincts. She should have insisted on accompanying Lucien to France. Perhaps if she had, he'd still be alive. But if Lucien hadn't gone to France, they might have never learned of Fouché's plot to kill Nelson this very night.

What did it matter now? She couldn't change the past. But she could save Vice-Admiral Nelson.

Her senses sharpened. She reached beneath her mourning garb and retrieved her pistol. She searched the crowd below and the boxes above. Everything still appeared normal, but normalcy was merely an illusion. If they weren't quick enough to foil an attempt on Nelson's life, all would be lost.

The vice-admiral was in plain sight, a perfect target. Would Stanton reach Simon and his men before it was too late? If not, she would have to warn Nelson herself somehow.

Her heart thumped wildly in her chest, her pulse a deafening, thunderous, roaring tide in her ears as an unethical idea made itself known to her. She *was* an acclaimed actress... If she could draw attention to herself, it was possible—only just—that her display could confuse the enemy long enough for the others to stop the attack. However, it would almost certainly ruin a dearly loved and thoroughly maligned woman's image—that of the vice-admiral's much-admired, steadfast wife, Frances.

Gillian swallowed and watched as Nelson stood erect, poised on the balls of his feet, contentedly absorbing the attention his delayed entrance provided. He was surrounded by three aides-de-camp. It was an unprecedented number for a man of his rank, but it was widely rumored to be compensation for the loss of his right arm and his partial blindness. He seemed to bask in the sea of acclamations echoing throughout the crowded amphitheater as the audience broke into applause. Calm in action, unreadable, he exhibited an illusion of calm to the public eye. Simon had once told her no one who served England was ever at ease. If that was the case, Nelson had to be on edge.

Nelson turned to his left and inclined his head to look down at Lady Hamilton. His smile revealed his generous, jovial nature and clear affection for the woman. The gesture tugged at Gillian's heartstrings. The beautiful and brown-haired Lady Hamilton looked impressively fit after delivering a baby in January, a child whispered to be Nelson's. She'd given him what his wife, Fanny, could not and had raised herself in Nelson's regard over and above any scandal their illicit affair produced. Might that have been her and Simon's fate if Simon hadn't convinced her to leave London with Lucien?

A knot of unwelcome tension gripped her as she observed the pair. What if Fouché's target wasn't Nelson at all, but the woman Nelson loved? She could think of no better way to break a man's spirit than to take from him that which he cherished most. If Nelson's permanent injuries had not succeeded in disarming the vice-admiral's spirit, would watching the woman he loved die in his arms have a different effect?

She didn't want to find out. A hush settled over the amphitheater as anticipation of another kind filled the air. Would Lord Nelson speak publicly? Gillian had no time to lose. She set the pistol on the side table nearby and leaned over the balcony, completely aware of the social repercussions that were sure to follow for the woman who the British people labeled "the right Lady Nelson." But bringing Lord Nelson's wife into this couldn't be helped. Nothing but saving Nelson mattered now.

"Nelson and Brontë," she shouted above the din in the most unladylike fashion. Yelling in public was never done, and her behavior would trigger Nelson's safeguards. In those three words, she'd identified herself as Lady Nelson, a woman who knew the vice-admiral signed every correspondence *Nelson and Brontë*, in honor of the title he'd earned in Sicily, Duke of Brontë. The general public wasn't aware of this, which would immediately earn Nelson's curiosity. "A gallant sight you are, standing there with a deadly blade close to your side."

Gillian prayed he understood her code: *Prepare for battle, my lord.*

A jaw-dropping hush overtook the crowd. The attention decreased the likelihood that Nelson's assassins would pick this opportune moment to strike.

"Dead foul!" The vice-admiral shouted, giving a quick nod to his aides, who surrounded Lady Hamilton. Without missing a beat, he bellowed, "Black does not become you, Fanny."

Stanton appeared at the auditorium entrance. He hurried to Simon's side, whispered in his ear, and then pointed to her. Simon's composure quickly altered.

Gillian continued the distraction to give Simon and Stanton and their guards enough time to locate Fouché's men. "It is *Lady* Nelson to all who know me here." A cheer rose up in the crowd at her ribald response, emboldening her. "I mourn for you, my dear husband. And if you value your life, you will unsheathe your blade."

Protect Lady Hamilton. You are both in grave danger.

"Fanny," Nelson replied, his baritone rising crisp and clear the way she'd imagined it would when calling to topmen aboard one of his ships. "I am sworn to defend all that I hold dear, including you."

"And defend those close to you, you must, my lord!" she said, nodding to Lady Hamilton. *The danger to you and your lady is very real.* "Make haste. You may turn a blind eye, but do not deafen your ears."

"I have sacrificed many things for my country, but I have not lost my hearing." Nelson curled his upper lip emphatically. "To be sure, there is no doing anything without trying it first."

Was he baiting his potential assassins? The vain man!

She scanned the audience, raised her gloved fist, shook it theatrically, and then placed it over her bosom to stall for time. The act symbolized a laborious and painful struggle going on inside her, melodrama the audience expected at the Theatre Royal.

"My heart's treasure, I am your Mrs. Billington, and

this—" she spread her arms wide "—is my *Love in a Village*." Billington was a Protestant actress whose husband was struck dead when Vesuvius erupted after her performance of the opera to a Catholic audience in Naples.

"I do not seek God's displeasure," Gillian said as Lady Nelson. "But your vanity, your love of glory and country . . . it grieves me sore. See how I mourn? Beware this night, my lord, for I fear it will get the better of you."

You are marked for death.

Her Shakespearean élan drew rowdy applause.

"You, my dear, have taken devotion to a questionable level." Nelson's voice boomed with unique force. "As you see—" he postured for the crowd "—I am alive and well."

Gillian tried to restrain her shock. He *was* baiting his assassins!

She cast her gaze around the well-lit theater again. "No one knows when Vesuvius will erupt," she responded, as movement in the box to her right caught her attention, making her skittish. "Beware the climb to loftier heights. No matter what befalls us, keep your feet firmly on the ground."

They might be upstairs. Be ready.

The crowd murmured in collective shock before cheering loudly.

Gillian curtsied, then backed into the shadows as a chair overturned in Box Four, the box next to hers. Gathering her wits, she put her ear to the wall and listened. There, she overheard enough French to put her into action. *"Tuez la!"*

Kill her!

Scuffling footsteps sounded, and Gillian lifted her skirts and removed the dagger she'd strapped to her leg. Quickly, she retrieved her pistol, wrapping her fingers around it. Now doubly armed, her nerves afire and anticipating the unexpected, she blew out the candles in Box Three.

Soon after, a man shoved his way inside. Likely disoriented by the darkness, he paused long enough that she figured he was letting his eyes adjust.

"What do you want?" she asked, thankful her dark clothing helped hide her. "This is a private box."

"A benefit to me, eh?" the man said in a French accent.

Another man whispered through the curtain, *"Tuez la."*

A knife gleamed in a fraction of a second before disappearing again into the darkness. "I'll take your voice, little songbird."

Gillian raised her pistol and cocked the trigger, gripping her dagger with her other hand. "Don't come any closer."

She heard him stop, his intake of breath, and felt him studying her, probably deciding whether or not she would truly kill him.

"I will not hesitate," she said, though they needed at least one of the men alive in order to glean information from them.

"Silly fool," he said, eyes narrowing. "What if you miss?"

Good God! What then? She couldn't possibly fire her weapon without injuring theatergoers in Box Two or possibly the Prince of Wales's box, creating panic below.

"Dépêche-toi!" the other man said. *Hurry up!* "The militia is coming."

He took an aggressive step toward her. "I *will* have satisfaction." He raised his blade.

She had no choice. She ducked, lowered to the ground, and swiped her dagger in a downward arc, slicing into his thighs. She scrambled to rise so she could sink the dagger deep into his chest if he came at her again.

Her aim was precise, however, and he howled, stumbled for purchase, and then fell over the box rail to the crowd below.

Screams rent the air. As she feared, the audience panicked.

"Botheration," she mumbled. That had not been something she'd even considered. Cautiously, she pulled back the curtain. Her attacker's partner appeared to be gone. She looked down the corridor, noting a large group of militiamen moving briskly toward the stairs.

Where to go? What to do? Gillian caught a slight movement to her left. There, her attacker's partner appeared. He held her gaze for agonizingly long seconds. He had not vanished as she'd first assumed but had returned to Box Four. Now that he'd been spotted by her, he attempted to blend in as several more gentlemen exited their boxes.

Not one to concede defeat—especially after what these men had tried to do, both to her and to Nelson—Gillian moved quickly after the Frenchman, thankful his tan beaver hat stood out in the crowd as she followed him down the back stairs. At the bottom of the landing, there was a door that led to Russell Street. Did he have transportation waiting for him there?

He glanced over his shoulder, and she quickly ducked behind a column. She counted to three before bolting after him, her heart hammering behind her ribs. Drury Lane's acting manager and actor John Philip Kemble allowed Nelson's would-be assassin to pass. He was ushering people out the door to prevent the frightened audience from creating a riot. Women wailed, and men shouted loudly, as fear that someone else would die this night drove them near the alcove exit where her quarry disappeared out the door.

Kemble spotted her. "Baroness!" he shouted, motioning to her with his hand.

She didn't have time to converse with Kemble. If she intended to catch the Frenchman, she'd have to avoid her old friend. Besides, the fact that he'd let the assassin go was something she couldn't think about yet. She rushed past the tall, somber actor, her heart drumming against her rib cage a she bolted out of reach.

"Brava, mia dolcissima," he called after her.

Outside, there was a collective murmur as heads bobbed and people turned to stare. She ignored the questioning looks, instead searching for the man in the tan beaver hat, who seemed to have disappeared again.

Gunfire erupted nearby, inciting the crowd into action. In the chaos, one hand clamped over her mouth, while an arm grasped her beneath her ribs. She bucked, kicking out her legs to ward off her attacker, but it was no use. She was pulled back toward the mews.

"This is for Claude, the man you killed inside the theater," a voice hissed against her ear. "And Mercier." He squeezed her tighter. "The man you killed in the woods."

Her lungs seized, but she tried not to panic as she felt her life begin to fade.

Relax. Let him think he has won, then attack.

Gillian lowered her arms, going limp.

One . . . Two . . . Three . . .

She stomped her heel on the top of the man's foot, startling him long enough to loosen his grip. Then she drove her elbow back into his stomach. He doubled over. She broke free and ran into another man's arms.

Had she miscounted? How many assassins were there?

She pulled back her fist, prepared to strike.

"Run, Gillian!" Simon ordered as he suddenly appeared and pushed her behind him.

"Simon . . . these men. They killed Lucien," she cried. "Lucien is dead."

Simon stilled and glanced at her for a fraction of a second. "Dead?"

She grabbed his arm. "Yes."

He eased her away from him and withdrew a sword from his cane with deadly calm. He advanced on the cornered assassin, discarding the silver-handled sheath beside him.

"This," he said, "is for the baron and his wife." Simon thrust the sword into the man's heart. "No mercy."

Gillian couldn't believe the ferocity of Simon's actions. They had needed to interrogate this man. She blinked and drew her head back stiffly before turning to run. Russell Street had changed little since she'd been gone, but she had changed, her view of the world had changed. She had to get away from all this death.

"Come," Simon said, appearing beside her. In her disoriented state, she allowed him to steer her toward a nearby carriage.

She seized Simon's arm once more. "This isn't over."

"No, it isn't." He hailed the driver. "Bolton Street."

"Aye, gov'na," the hackney replied.

Simon opened the carriage door. "Quick! Get inside. It isn't safe for you here. God only knows how many French sympathizers you might have angered in the theater tonight."

She glanced around her. "Where is the admiral? Did he escape injury? How did *you* get here so fast?"

He didn't answer, just continued urging her into the carriage. "Come on," he said.

Knowing she was safer with Simon than she was alone on the streets, Gillian agreed. She stepped into the carriage and took a seat on the squabs. Simon followed. He tapped on the ceiling and the equipage jerked into motion.

"The admiral," she tried again, "is he . . . ?"

"Rest assured, the admiral and his lady are safe, thanks to you."

Gillian nodded, her heartbeat pulsing in her neck. Surely, after all she'd been through—the danger, the horror—she could finally relax. But she couldn't. The man she'd once loved sat before her. She tucked her hands in the folds of her skirts to hide how badly they shook.

Simon leaned forward until a strand of moonlight illuminated his expressionless face. "Why didn't you tell me Admiral Nelson's life was in jeopardy?"

She occupied herself by looking out the window. She'd obeyed her husband in all things, done what she'd promised, and taken the necessary risks to save a man vital to England's success. That was what she and Lucien had always done. They'd followed orders without asking why. But Simon didn't know she was a spy—not yet.

She suspected Lucien had sent her to Stanton because he knew a meeting between her and Simon might cloud both of their judgments, and he'd be right indeed. Even after five years, she felt her heartstrings stir an unruly awareness in her body and soul. 'Twas a feeling she'd fight to her bitter end. Nothing good could come of it.

His shoulders tensed as he tightened his grip on the handle his cane. "Don't you trust me anymore?"

Heat rose to her face, and she inhaled a stabilizing breath. He frowned, his brows level above his searching eyes. She knew full well that without Simon's intervention, she might be dead on the street this very moment.

"I used to trust you," she readily admitted.

Simon nodded. "I broke your trust . . ." His admission settled over her like a blanket of snow—cold, exact, haunting. "But I did not lie about my circumstances in the end. I confessed the truth about my betrothal."

At his voice, heat thundered through her veins against her wishes. She swallowed. "Yes. You did. And the vital lesson I learned has sustained me for many years. One can hardly believe the most trustworthy of people these days."

Gillian glanced away. It did neither of them any good to dwell on the damage done to their relationship. Enough time had passed that she certainly didn't know Simon anymore. Nor did she want to. Hadn't she already been through enough in the past two days? She was thoroughly spent and eager for a safe place to rest her weary head. She didn't want to argue.

He crossed his arms over his chest. "You didn't come to see an opera, did you?"

"I—" Her hands began to tremble. "What you believe doesn't matter, my lord."

"Everything about you matters to me."

His leather-and-spice scent took her back to another time and place. His splendidly proportioned body owned the seat across from her, making her remember things that would only do her emotional harm. How frustrating it was to be confined together in such tight quarters where his knee brushed against hers!

His touch sent another scorching heat below her skirts to places a decent woman—let alone a widow—dared not acknowledge. She closed her eyes, trying to put his devilishly handsome face out of her mind. But like a bird in a gilded cage, she was good and truly caught.

The carriage wheels jostled over the cobblestones. What was she to do now? She bit back several tremulous gasps.

"Forgive me," he said suddenly, snapping her out of her doldrums.

Her gaze locked with his. "For what, my lord?"

"For my past indiscretions."

She grimaced. This was exactly what she'd feared. Being alone with Simon and being forced to relive the past, to acknowledge her feelings for him.

"For the way I disappointed you," he said. She looked away as Simon cleared his throat. "Do not shut me out, Gillian. May we please talk like two civilized people?"

"We were more than that," she said, turning toward him again, "and you know it."

"I know . . ." His expression softened. "There are many things still left unsaid between us."

"Your confession was quite clear," she disagreed. "I need

no further explanation."

"I meant—" he cleared his throat "—only to discover what happened to the baron." Simon regarded her closely. The intensity of his stare was breaking down carefully constructed walls she'd erected around her heart in order to fulfill the vow she'd made to Lucien. "How did he die?"

Her brow furrowed. "I am weary, Simon."

He nodded. "And I am trying to be considerate. But I cannot know what kind of trouble you are in unless you tell me what happened in Kent." He removed his hat and set it on the seat beside him. "Gillian, the past is gone. Times as they are, I take it upon myself to think only of today and what tomorrow will bring. I am concerned for your safety. I mean nothing untoward. Please tell me what happened."

How did she break the news to this man, who'd insisted she marry a man of Lucien's caliber? She was barely able to muster enough strength to breathe. It was too much too soon.

"My husband," she said on a half breath, "is dead."

"And I killed a man because of it." Simon leaned forward and perched on the edge of his seat. His dark earnest eyes sought hers as he quickly took her hands in his. "I'm sorry. I know you well enough to know you would never interrupt a performance unless it was life or death." The steady cadence of his voice began to calm her. She yearned for comfort, for someone to talk to about what she'd seen and done. "That was a very brave thing you just did."

Was it? She'd killed two men—one intentionally, and one while trying to protect herself. She would have to answer for that someday.

"No braver than Lucien going to France to retrieve information that would save the admiral's life in the first place," she said. Lucien's determination to beat the sodding Frenchman Fouché at his own game had come to an end. She placed her hand over her heart. The fool organ fought for control over her body, almost stealing her breath. "My husband was murdered, Simon. He died . . . in my arms."

"Christ!" He studied her for a disquieting moment, then squeezed her hand, his comforting touch eroding her defenses. "Forgive me, but the baron was a master spy with the willpower of a saint. I assume he was followed?"

"Yes." *Followed and hunted down like a worthless animal.* "His horse returned to our home and then took me to him."

Simon chuckled. "He never would tell me how he trained Polaris."

"I am thankful the cunning beast took me straight to him. Had I gotten there any later . . ." She gazed into his eyes. "I cannot bear to think of what it would have been like for Lucien to die alone. Or that he would have died in vain." Her words drifted off as sadness flooded her.

I cannot fall to pieces in front of him. *I will not.*

"Did he suffer?" His voice exuded deadly calm, but it was an illusion. Gillian knew Simon well enough to know he took great pride in hiding the depth of his emotions.

Tears filled her eyes. "He'd been shot in the stomach."

Simon flinched. "A man can linger in agony for hours with such a wound."

"By the time I found him, he'd lost too much blood. God knows how long it had been since he'd been wounded . . . There was blood in Polaris's mane." Once those words came, she was unable to stop. She told Simon everything—how she'd found Lucien, how she'd killed his attacker, a man the stranger in the alley had called Mercier—trying to purge herself of the horror. The only way her assailant could have known was if he'd followed Gillian and her maid, Cora, to London. "We were followed. I am certain of it."

Simon quietly listened. He lifted her veil and tossed her hat aside, cradling her face in his hands. His thumbs caressed her cheeks, gently soothing her. And when wild grief finally racked her body and she bowed over, slumping in despair, he moved to sit beside her and wrapped her in his arms.

Gillian clung to him then, burrowing against his hard-muscled chest, absorbing his strength as her heartache and pain spilled forth. A spy always knew the end might come, but nothing had prepared her for the reality of Lucien's death, the anguish and the loss she'd feel.

He held her to him, one hand in her hair, the other against the small of her back. It felt natural—right somehow. "You've been through a terrible ordeal, and you're exhausted," he said, killing her with kindness. "Where will you go now? What will you do?"

She pulled away and sat back, wiping her tears with the back of her hand. It was time she faced that her life would never be the same. There was nothing right about the way she was drawn to Simon. She forced a smile. "What any widow does, I suppose, when the man she relied on is gone."

"Forgive me," he said, reaching out to take her hand in his, "I am not schooled on these matters, and thankfully so. What does a widow do?"

His entreaty sank deep into her spirit. Yet, fearing for her mortal soul, Gillian recoiled from the man she'd once loved and lost twice now. She wasn't too far gone to presume that any romantic notions she'd once had could materialize. After all, Simon was still married.

Screams of frustration welled in the back of her throat, and a tide of weariness and despair took hold. "Where is this carriage going?"

"Number Eleven Bolton Street," he said.

Bolton Street wasn't on a main thoroughfare, but rather, it branched off Piccadilly. She shook her head to clear it, grabbed her hat, and plunked it atop her head, positioning the skewed veil over her face to keep him from seeing her clearly.

"I should return to Kent."

Nausea washed over her. What was he thinking? She needed to get out of the carriage as soon as possible. Simon lived at Number Seventeen Curzon Street. Traveling with him to places unknown wasn't a good idea, especially in her present state.

"Kent?" He shook his head. "It isn't safe for you there. Not anymore."

She shrank back, astounded by the sincerity in Simon's voice. "Who are you to decide my fate?"

"What I mean to say is this," he began again, slow and smooth. "More men will be sent to finish Fouché's work. If you return to Kent, it will not take long for anyone to trace you back there. After your courageous display inside the Theatre Royal, I have no doubt you are now on their list. No, my sweet. You cannot go home. That is the first place Fouché's men will look for you."

A bitter cold despair consumed her. She and Lucien had made their life in Kent. "But Lucien . . ." she said. "There was no time to . . . I left him lying in the wood, Simon! He deserves a proper funeral and burial."

Simon stiffened and then nodded. "And he shall get one." His tone was edged with steel but oddly gentle. "I give you my word as a gentleman."

"Gentleman or no, I am no longer your concern," she reminded him.

His gaze softened as it met hers. "If not mine, then whose?"

Six

"Jealous in honor, sudden and quick in quarrel,
Seeking the bubble reputation
Even in the cannon's mouth. And then the justice . . ."
~William Shakespeare, As You Like It

WHO WOULD PROTECT the baroness if Simon did not? She had no family left to her credit, and the man who'd taken care of her was dead. But that wasn't what shocked him the most. Somehow, Gillian had possessed the wherewithal to miraculously kill two assassins and incite another to attempt to kill her in public.

"How did you manage it, Gillian?" The awe in his voice gave too much away and didn't properly express his concern.

"Manage what, my lord?" she had the audacity to ask as she moved to the opposite seat.

The carriage paused momentarily and then jolted forward, horses clip-clopping once more on the cobblestone streets as the carriage made its way toward their destination—his newly outfitted townhouse on Bolton Street in Mayfair.

"We are not in the theater, Gillian. Don't play coy with me." Fate had thrown them together once more, and the old masks needed to be cast aside. If anyone in this world cared about her, it was Simon. He waited patiently for her to answer. She didn't. "How did you evade Nelson's assassins?"

"Practice," she said simply.

Her confession vibrated through him. *She* was a spy? The baron had tricked him!

But it all made sense now—the ease with which Chauncey had collected information at soirees, the logistics of being in two places at one time. Damn the man's bones for bringing Gillian into his dangerous life!

Looking back now, Simon realized he'd been a fool. In his quest to protect Gillian, he'd arranged for her to marry a French expatriate, a spy whose forays into France only increased her chances of being put in harm's way, of being used as leverage against Chauncey. Is that why the baron had recruited and trained Gillian? The only reason she had been able to escape Fouché's men was because her husband had taught her how to survive in a world of espionage and deceit. It made her far more valuable and more unlike any other woman Simon had ever known.

Over the past five years, he'd tried to forget Gillian. He'd even convinced himself he'd done the right thing by her. He was a man of honor who valued promises, and he'd promised to love and protect her until the day he died. But he had broken that vow by agreeing to marry another woman, a woman he didn't love, for his family's sake. He'd tried to move on. Thought he had, in fact. Now he understood his brother, Byron, the Duke of Throckmorton's tortured existence. Rock, as Simon called his brother, had never been the same since his beloved wife, Lady Olivia Throckmorton, had died at the hands of pirates. He had nearly lost his daughter, Lady Constance, in the same tragedy.

The thought of losing the only woman he'd ever loved, as Rock had, chilled him to his marrow. "You could have fallen out of that box to your death," he pointed out.

Streetlamps flickered as they passed, and tension thickened inside the carriage.

She clenched her jaw. "But I did not."

Her rebellion terrified him. It meant she was numb to danger, likely having faced it many a time and come out on the winning end. And her refusal to let him back into her life when she needed him most was a prime example of how much more independent—and stubborn—she'd become. He simply could not bear to lose Gillian twice. But that was what awaited him if he let her leave. He knew he couldn't stop her if it was what she truly wanted, but she *was* in danger. Gone was the stiff, unyielding chit he'd met in 1795 during a political fiasco of a play, *Venice Preserv'd* produced by Sheridan and Kemble.

"You have no right," she said, breaking the silence, "to march back into my life and take control of it. I assure you, I am capable of taking care of myself."

"I've borne witness to that effect." Simon frowned. "I never meant to imply otherwise. It takes admirable skill to outwit one's enemy."

"One simply has to know who the enemy is," she said.

Simon stared at her, transfixed. Chauncey had been a good man, an even better agent. He'd also been one of Simon's most trusted confidants. They'd worked together on numerous cases, the most memorable of which was James Hadfield's assassination attempt on King George III, and more recently with d'Auvergne, securing informants privy to Napoleon's activities in France, infiltrating Saint-Malo to sabotage pirate ships, and helping to undermine France's monetary system. Theirs had been a covert mission at an opportune time when Nelson had been charged with protecting the Channel.

Damn it! Chauncey's loss cost him plenty; in fact, it left him blind.

Flexibility saved lives, and difficult times called for extreme measures. "Your returning to Kent is out of the question, Gillian."

"Where, pray, am I expected to go, then?"

Now they were getting somewhere. The well-bred lady who sat before him was a baroness, a powerful enigma who was secure in her shell. Her skills could provide Nelson's Tea with the feminine persuasion they lacked . . .

He rolled his shoulders, trying to ease his nerves. Did he really want to recruit Gillian? Loss was an insistent beast with claws that refused to disengage; loss was at the heart of every step he took in this life of wits and brawn. But if Simon achieved his goals, the world would be a safer place to live.

Yes. Gillian would be an asset to the vice-admiral's crew. Simon should know—he was a skilled politician. He'd survived hand-to-hand combat with the Malouin Robert Surcouf, and Frenchmen and Spaniards alike. He'd argued with King George III and the Prince of Wales, and lived to tell the tale. He'd even bantered with Admirals Duncan, Nelson, and Cochrane as if he were their equal.

Loyalty, honor, and duty—these were personality traits he looked for in operatives. A man in his position couldn't ask for sacrifices if he wasn't willing to make them. And oh, his sacrifices had been great, indeed. They would be even greater if he persuaded Gillian to join their ranks and had to interact with her regularly.

As the carriage jostled along the road, passing the Royal Mews and then St. James Square, Simon tapped his cane impatiently on the floorboard, anxious to discuss his idea with Gillian.

She sat before him like frothy ale to a sailor who'd not seen a tavern in months. She was an inaccessible rose, her beauty his bane and her thorns piercing his heart in an ever-tightening vise. Was she aware of her power over him? That, at one time, he'd loved her more than life itself? That he'd always love her?

It was that very same love that motivated him to see her safely settled. But few were the ways he could reveal the true state of his emotions. He'd married another, and because of it, he didn't deserve her forgiveness.

"Gillian," he said, now stewing in agony.

"My lord," she said sharply, as if attempting to distance herself from him. "We have come far, you and I. But we both know familiarizing ourselves with each other is not wise."

He sighed. "Very well, Baroness." He inclined his head. "I shall make your situation clear. You've made enemies. You need a safe haven—protection." Light from a streetlamp illuminated her gaze momentarily. Deep brown eyes searched his soul. "Protection I'm more than willing to give."

She lifted her chin. "You and I both know what you did the last time you were faced with this choice."

"Perhaps another advantageous marriage would—"

"Out of the question," she snapped.

Simon lifted his cane and tapped on the ceiling. The driver responded to the prompt, and the carriage rolled to a stop.

"Why?" he asked, determined to make her see reason. "Fouché's men are ruthless."

"I have seen their wickedness firsthand," she said. "I do not need to be reminded."

"Then why are you so willing to tempt death when you have everything to live for? The baron was a good man—a great man, in fact—but you are a young, beautiful, intelligent woman with plenty of options."

"Do not try to sway me—"

"I could never do that. Not after . . ." He cleared his throat. "I speak from the heart when I say your safety takes precedence over whatever has happened between us." He shifted uncomfortably in his seat. Pride niggled at the back of his brain, threatening to get the best of him. He removed his top hat and raked his hands through his hair. "We need a woman of your—" he fought for the right words, inclining his head toward her widow's garb "—talents."

Her frown made him want to melt into the woodwork. "We?" she asked.

Was that the only word she'd heard? Deuce it all, she'd grown more stubborn, more astute over the years. His heart swelled, filling the space behind his ribs. Chauncey had taken a young, indulgent girl and filled her with determination, heart, and spunk, making her hard as steel. Gillian's independence was a fascinating thing to behold. And it scared him.

Simon swallowed the heavy lump wedged in his throat. "You would be a magnificent addition to the admiral's crew."

"His crew?" Gillian's brow lifted. "You cannot be serious."

"I assure you, I am." He waved aside her incredulity, confident he could persuade her to accept a place in his world, even though it frightened him to think of her in danger. "If the baron trained you, you know what it is that we do. And if you know what we do, that makes you either an asset or a detriment to us." He paused. "The way I see it, joining us will allow you to further your independence and challenge yourself more than becoming an isolated country mouse, someone's governess, or a merchant struggling to make ends meet would." She leaned back and closed her eyes, almost as if in defeat. He watched her closely, unable to ignore his racing pulse. "Of course, if Chauncey's death has robbed you of spirit, I will be happy to—"

"There is nothing you can do." She opened her eyes and stared at him. "Why are you so insistent?"

"We could be partners, Gillian."

"I had a brilliant partner."

"In every sense?" *Bollocks!* Why had he asked such a thing? After earning her love and then tearing her heart apart by announcing he was betrothed to another, he'd lost that right.

She shrugged dismissively. "Every sense but one."

He rubbed the back of his hand across his mouth. "Only one?"

"*Mais oui,*" she said, reverting to French as if born to it.

What other skills did she have?

She sighed. "You cannot expect me to speak it."

Simon shook his head. He yearned to uncover all Gillian's secrets, one by everlasting one. But now wasn't the time to reclaim his foolish youth. The baron lay dead—but not forgotten—in a forest in Kent.

Simon tapped the ceiling with his cane and sank back into the squabs as the carriage vaulted forward, regaining its normal tempo. The vehicle's suspension rattled. Gillian closed her eyes once more. He studied her face, comparing it to the one he'd compartmentalized in his memories, opening the doors to a part of his past he'd kept under lock and key. Her rosewood scent infiltrated his senses. Her dainty hands were set in her lap, just above the juncture of her thighs. He stared at her gloved fingers, watching for movement, nearly driving himself mad.

"You said you and the baron were partners in every way but one," he pressed again. She opened her eyes, those very same eyes he remembered melting like honey whenever he'd pressed his mouth to hers. "Did you love him?"

"What would make you ask such a question, Simon?" He'd shocked her, perhaps even repulsed her. "Of course I loved Lucien!" she cried, as if the hounds of Hades were going to maul her to death for vowing anything less.

Simon knew he'd gone too far. And yet, a wicked sense of arrogance burned inside him. He couldn't stop wondering how happy Gillian had been with the baron while Simon had watched his wife's health wane. "Were you . . . intimate?"

Gillian gaped at him. "I will not dignify that question with an answer." She turned her face away, focusing her attention out the carriage window. Her refusal settled over him like ash.

"Gillian." He moved beside her, the carriage shifting beneath his weight. He took her hand in his and squeezed it lightly, waiting an eternity for her to look back at him. His patience was rewarded when ever so slowly, she glanced up through her lashes. He'd dreamed of this moment, of perusing her features at his leisure. A twinge of guilt stabbed him. If he allowed it, Gillian would surely be the end of him. And yet he couldn't detach himself, no matter how hard he tried. "I wish things could have been different for us."

She inhaled, the sound hypnotic, seductive, and practically driving him over the edge. "But they weren't."

"No. They weren't." He moved closer and lifted her featherlight veil. His senses on high alert, his entire body attuned to hers, feeling more alive than he had in years, he traced her wet tears with his fingers. "Nothing I do can take away your pain. Chauncey was a good man."

"He was. Oh, Simon." Tears welled in Gillian's eyes. She shivered, then sank into his arms.

He held her close, breathing in her scent, luxuriating in the feel of her silky hair against his chin. He stroked her hair, a dull ache throbbing in his chest. Life was cruel, and fate was an unkind master. He wanted her, needed her, as he was struck with the reality of how different things would have been if Gillian hadn't escaped the gendarmes.

"I will never forget him," she said, her voice breaking.

"I pray you never do."

Her sobs came out in a choking rush as she clung to him, her nails digging into his arms. She cried out her husband's name, and then pummeled Simon with her fists. He took her anger, accepted each blow, and continued to hold her tight, comforting her and sharing her sorrow, until she quieted and relaxed against him.

When he spoke again, the truth shot through him like a musket ball. "Chauncey," he started, "once said he'd fled France to help his people. He never once refused to go back to France when the Admiralty needed eyes inside enemy lines. He did everything that was requested of him and more. So much more."

What man would agree to marry a woman another man loved? The baron had done so. He'd kept his word. He'd safeguarded Gillian, given her stability, and nurtured her spirit. Simon would have most assuredly broken her if she'd stayed and become his mistress. He was who he was—no excuses, no more lies.

"Everything?" she repeated, her brows knitting together as she lifted her face to meet his.

"Yes," he said, stabbed with guilt as her grief-stricken eyes impaled him. She felt so right in his arms, as if she were part of him, an extension of his soul. Her half-parted lips begged for him to chase away her sorrow. Part of him was eager to assist her, to help her forget the horrors she'd experienced and taste her. "And we shared something else—wanting something we could not have."

She blinked. "Lucien wanted to destroy Napoleon."

"As do I." He nodded. "But that is not all I've wanted and you know it."

"That is life," she said. "There will always be something out of reach." She placed a finger over his lips. "You are an honorable man, Simon. You did what you thought was right for me, for both of us. And you are still married. I understand." She paused. "I've always understood." She caressed his cheek. "There will never be a day I won't fondly remember what we shared."

The iron restraints that had gripped him from the moment he'd watched Gillian marry the baron burst open.

Sensations he'd forgotten poured over him as his heart began to burn, igniting him with unruly fire. He didn't deserve Gillian's compassion, or even to be loved. He was a man of action, a man who did what needed to be done, no matter the consequences to himself or anyone else. He longed to believe he was the man she claimed him to be. Succumbing, he pulled her into his arms and hugged her close.

Enveloped in darkness, they traveled in silence, him holding her, stroking her arm. Fate warred against them. War. Danger. Time. He'd abandoned Gillian to marry the woman his family had chosen for him, Lady Edwina Landon-Fitzhugh, a woman who fought each day to survive to the next. She'd never complained about his frequent voyages on HMS *Agamemnon* or the countless hours he spent helping Henry Dundas circumvent diplomatic tides. Edwina's constancy was no match for her ill-health, however, and the children who'd died stillborn.

He could not abandon the woman who'd struggled in vain to make him happy at the expense of her own happiness. Torn between two women, Simon resignedly closed his eyes.

The carriage stopped.

Gillian settled back on the squabs and wiped her tear-stained cheeks. She straightened her coiffure and put her hat back on her head. "Where are we?" she asked.

"Number Eleven Bolton Street. My new townhouse."

"You cannot be serious." Gillian became restless. "Surely you do not intend for me to stay here. It would be unseemly."

His mind reeled, and he stared back at her, baffled, as the air turned frigid. Only moments ago she'd leaned on him to ease her grief. "You have nowhere else to go," he said.

She turned away from him, but he would not be shut out. Of course, there were other places she could go. He knew that well enough. None, however, could provide the protection she needed. Until his men reported back to him—

and he was confident Fouché's men were not a danger to her—it was his responsibility to protect Gillian.

He reached for her, grabbed her chin, and gently prodded her to look at him. Not another moment would go by without him speaking his mind. He had this one chance to persuade Gillian to work with them. Nelson's Tea needed a woman like her, someone who could go where others could not. "There are bigger things at work here than you know."

"I'm quite aware of what is happening in the world, my lord."

"All right, then. I *need* you," he finally admitted.

Her laughter sounded half crazed. "*You* do not need me. You are a distinguished member of the Admiralty. You are a duke's brother—and need I remind you that you're married."

"No." He stiffened as though he'd been struck. "I do not need to be reminded."

"Then I can see no reason for me to stay here. It would not be socially acceptable."

"Not if this townhouse is yours," he said. He tilted her head toward the entrance. "Think of it. You will be able to continue Chauncey's work, make a difference, and be a part of something bigger than yourself. Admiral Nelson did not just come to London to attend the theater or speak in Parliament. He came to form a covert group of mercenaries charged with protecting England's shores. And Number Eleven Bolton Street is where it will begin."

"Nelson's Tea?" she asked, surprising him. At his nod, she continued, "Lucien told me. When will this take place?"

"Soon," he said, astonished by the resonant hint of pride in his own voice. He studied her momentarily. "Join us. I want you to be a part of what we're about to accomplish, Gillian. Take your husband's place. Your talents will be put to optimum use." He made no effort to conceal his allusion to her feminine attributes. They needed someone who could infiltrate Society and wheedle secrets from the *ton* without anyone being the wiser. And who better to play the game than an independent woman with a title, such as an available widow like Gillian? Her acting experience could also be beneficial.

"What you ask—" she paused "—carries great weight. And after what I've just done to Admiral Nelson . . ." She held her hand up to her neck. "Why, I doubt he would sanction my participation."

Simon threw his head back and laughed his first genuine laugh in ages. "Believe me when I say you are exactly what the admiral needs: someone who isn't influenced by his larger-than-life persona."

She chewed her bottom lip, making it grow plump, red, and far more tempting than was proper. Simon cleared his throat and diverted his eyes.

"There are matters that must be discussed," she said softly.

"But you agree to stay here, at least for tonight, where it's safe?"

"Do I have your word you will stay elsewhere?"

Was that her only concession?

"Do not worry. Everything will be aboveboard. You have my word." She'd agreed to one night, which was more than he'd hoped for. "I will return home as soon as you are settled."

"I will stay," she said, a bitter edge of determination in her tone, "until I'm confident our past will not be problematic."

"I'm not asking for anything you cannot and will not give," he clarified. "I am a married man. I know that well enough, and I still feel as I did five years ago: I would never demean you by making you my mistress." He cocked his brow, wondering if the subtle confession that he still loved her would change her mind. He wouldn't blame her, if it did. But he *needed* her. "With or without you, England's future depends on the men and women willing to sacrifice themselves for the greater good."

She placed her hand on his sleeve, a dim flush racing across her face feverishly fast. "And you will go home to her? Where you belong?"

Devil take it, he didn't want to leave Gillian. He studied the dark lashes that swept down over her delicate cheekbones, and her full rosy mouth. It was all he could do to speak. "Yes."

"Then I wish you safe journey," she said.

A footman left the townhouse entrance and opened the carriage door, fracturing the moment. Goodayle, chief protector of his secrets and his acting butler, stood right behind him.

"Good evening, my lord." Goodayle bowed as Simon exited the carriage and turned to offer Gillian his hand.

Once she was firmly on the ground, he looked to his butler. "Goodayle, may I present Baroness Chauncey. She will be staying at Number Eleven until further notice."

Goodayle bowed again. "If there is anything you need, my lady, you only have to ask."

"Thank you, Goodayle," Gillian said with a nod.

"Goodayle and I served on the *Agamemnon* together," Simon whispered as he escorted her to the townhouse stoop behind Goodayle, hoping to reassure her that she would be safe. "Though he may not look it, he is more than a butler."

"The Honorable Sidney Wittingham at your service, Baroness," Goodayle said.

"You are titled, and yet you perform the tasks of servant?" she asked, then glanced at Simon. "That isn't seemly."

"To the first, a viscount's son holds no title. To the second, some causes are worth their disguises, Baroness,"

Goodayle explained. "I can think of no better way to serve my king than to ensure Lord Danbury's success. No one will infiltrate Number Eleven unless I allow it."

Gillian nodded, then straightened her spine as she peered at Simon. "You have thought of everything, it appears."

No. He hadn't been prepared for her. He swallowed and forced a smile. "I leave you in Goodayle's dependable care," was all he could say.

"Will you not be joining her, my lord?" Goodayle asked, his brow cocked curiously.

The temptation to do so, to spend more time in Gillian's company, tugged at him like a riptide. But he could no sooner stay than tame the ocean's currents. "No," he said, forcing the word from his mouth as he whirled away and walked back to the carriage.

"Thank you, my lord," she called after him. "For . . . everything."

Everything. The word reminded him that the baron had done all that he'd asked of him and more, including provide Gillian the means to protect herself. Now, here she was, though under horrific circumstances. She was a bright, glorious star, beckoning mariners away from hazardous rocks. He looked back over his shoulder at her in silent expectation. "You're welcome, Baroness."

A tingling sensation coiled in the pit of his stomach. He'd long valued his ability to remain emotionally detached, but now his senses were shouting in uproar. Surely the adventurous undertaking to thwart an assassination attempt on Vice-Admiral Nelson was the cause. And yet, he was powerless to resist staring at the woman who'd once stolen his heart. She'd appeared like a bolt of lightning, jarring him out of his meditative state. He'd forgotten the intensity of desire, of the need to stake his claim on something that wasn't his. What he felt for Gillian now had nothing to do with reason and everything to do with a reawakening passion, the very thing his marriage to Edwina lacked.

He cleared his throat. "Goodayle is my man, Baroness. He'll see you good and settled. Whatever you need, direct your requests to him." He motioned to the hackney. "Curzon Street. Two ticks." The hackneys he used at Drury Lane knew to double the distance to his home when he gave them that order. Sometimes he needed the privacy the interior of the carriage provided to think. He stepped into the carriage and settled back on the squabs as the footman closed to door behind him.

What was he to do now? His damned traitorous heart hammered against his ribs as the carriage set off, taking him farther away from the woman he'd spent too many years without.

Seven

"In fair round belly with good capon lined,
With eyes severe and beard of formal cut,
Full of wise saws and modern instances . . ."
~William Shakespeare, As You Like It

GILLIAN QUESTIONED THE rightness of her actions as she followed Goodayle inside Number Eleven. At least, her decision to accept Simon's sanctuary would give her time to properly consider his offer to join Nelson's Tea, given Lucien's death, the attempt on Vice-Admiral Nelson's life, and her near escape from Fouché's men. Danger was what she had known for the past five years, but was it how she wanted to live the rest of her life? She had a chance to start over, to leave behind her past loves and memories of what could have been. Was that what she really wanted?

"This way, if you please," Goodayle said, his tone patient as she came to a stop in the middle of the foyer and took off her hat. "Watch your step."

"Thank you, Goodayle." Immediately, she took in the layout of the townhouse. Its magnificent wrought iron staircase ascended to the upper floors and a balcony, and a chandelier hung high overhead, its crystal prisms reflecting light that gave a subdued golden hue to everything in view.

To her left, a set of double doors suggested a parlor, library, or study would be found there, and a hallway led past the staircase and farther into the townhouse. The latter would require investigation.

"This way, Baroness," Goodayle said. "You may have guessed by now, given your association with Lord Danbury, that this is not a regular townhouse."

She tilted her head. "How so?"

Goodayle cut his gaze to her as if assessing whether or not she could be trusted. "Architectural adjustments needed to be made to the interior. I believe, in time, you will find them satisfactory."

"What kind of adjustments?" she asked. If she was going to be part of Simon's clandestine group of mercenaries, there were things she needed to know. "And how long has Lord Danbury been renovating?"

Goodayle shrugged. "He began refurbishments shortly after Georges Cadoudal failed to kill Napoleon with a cart bomb last Christmas Eve."

"Hmm." She imagined the place to plot clandestine action was better suited to Whitehall, the military headquarters in Westminster. "Has he been recruiting men for Nelson's Tea for quite some time?"

His deep chuckle helped put her at ease. "The idea was birthed on the *Agamemnon*."

"I see." But she didn't. Simon began working with Henry Dundas and the House of Lords after he'd left HMS *Agamemnon* in 1795. Had it taken him over five years to choose the right men, or had he been forced to wait until circumstances between France and England had worsened? She smoothed the lace veil on her hat to hide her nervousness. Simon had never talked about his naval career with her. "So you and Lord Danbury served aboard the *Agamemnon* together?"

"Aye." He grew serious as he moved across the black-and-white marble-tiled floor toward the stairs.

She observed Goodayle keenly. If Lucien had taught her anything, it was to recognize character traits that coincided with good or evil. Sometimes the lines intersected; other times they were ripped asunder. She suspected Goodayle fell into another category altogether. His dedication, devotion, and determination hinted not at servitude but at the air of a gentleman shirking all but duty, honor, and country.

"Those were dark times, my lady," he said as he came to a stop at the bottom of the stairs. "Toulon, Calvi, Genoa, and the Hyères Islands. We've been through hell together."

She stared at the candlestick Goodayle held in his hand, hypnotized by its flickering flame. "The admiral lost sight in his right eye at Calvi, didn't he? Were you and Lord Danbury there?"

He nodded. "French shot kicked sand into the admiral's face. Still, he insisted on leading the assault, refusing to seek help. He was permanently blinded as a result. We've never forgotten his selfless act." He motioned to the stairs. "Follow me, please."

She fell into step behind him. "The *Agamemnon* played a part in the mutiny at the Nore, is that correct?"

"We weren't aboard her at the time." He stopped to stare at her. "The admiral was reassigned to HMS *Captain*. As we were all to be dispersed to other ships, he requested that Lord Danbury and I follow him there." He moved slowly up the steps, allowing her time to pick up her skirts. "The *Captain* was sent to Portugal, earning the admiral acclaim at Cape St. Vincent. A good ship, she was, too. Gave her all to defeat the Spanish. From her decks, we had the distinct honor of watching Admiral Nelson board the Spanish ship, the *San Nicolas*, winning its surrender." He paused, frowning. "I've never seen a man so driven. It isn't an easy task to follow a man like Admiral Nelson."

"I am not acquainted with the admiral. He appears amiable enough to me," she said.

"Oh, you misunderstand, my lady. I refer to the loss of his sight, of watching him suffer recurring bouts of malaria, and a musket ball wound that shattered his right arm. He ordered the surgeon to amputate his arm so he could rejoin the fight. If it weren't for John Sykes, who saved Nelson's life twice by being in the wrong place at the right time . . ."

"Of course," she said as they mounted the stairs. "'Greater love hath no man than this, that a man lay down his life for his friends.' Noble sacrifices predating war between France and England. Gripping and necessary, indeed."

Goodayle stopped and looked down at her. "You have sacrificed, as well, my lady." Tears welled in her eyes, and he cleared his throat before continuing up the staircase. "We have all given up something we cherished. Admiral Nelson is just one of the good men who've given their lives and pieces of themselves to defeat Napoleon."

Silence descended upon them as they climbed the staircase past gilded-framed landscapes of men hunting with large hounds to a landing where the wrought iron artistry curved along the balcony. Before her, lining the walls along the next set of stairs, were the unseeing eyes of officers in the Horse Guards, lords of Parliament and their consorts, and members of King George III's court.

At the top of the next landing, the corridor was dark, save for the light coming from Goodayle's candle. Gillian counted her footsteps, memorizing every door and corner for later use, an old habit that enabled her to escape whenever necessary.

Shadows danced along the walls as Goodayle stopped

beside a door. "This will be your room, Baroness."

"If we are to be acquainted, please call me Gillian," she said, her bombazine skirts swishing in the eerie quiet as he led the way.

"You are most generous, but I cannot." He shook his head. "If we are to work together, it wouldn't be proper. Appearances are everything, my lady." His square jaw grew more pronounced, hinting at the man's impressive stubbornness. "No matter what you may think, I took an oath to protect Lord Danbury. I gave up my name, and I must behave like a servant at all times if I am to fool anyone of my true heritage. One slipup could mean the difference between life and death—for you, for me, and for Lord Danbury and his family."

"I understand." She did. More than he likely realized. "How are Lord Danbury's brother, niece, and—" she paused "—his wife?"

"His Grace and Lady Constance are well." He stiffened. "Lady Danbury, however, is gravely ill."

Her eyes widened. "Ill? What has happened? Lord Danbury made no mention of it to me." But of course, why would he? Five years ago, he had married another woman, knowing it had broken her heart.

"He's a very private man, my lady." Goodayle backed away, refusing to say more, and motioned to the door. "Is there anything you need before I close up the house for the night?"

"That will not be necessary," she said, stewing on the news that Simon's wife was ill. A sense of dread filled her. She didn't want Simon to lose his wife, especially not after she'd lost Lucien and understood firsthand what it felt like. She grabbed the door handle with trembling fingers. What was wrong with Lady Danbury? Was there anything she could do to help? She had a good grasp of medicinal herbs. Perhaps if she could examine the woman . . .

What are you thinking? Get control of yourself. Simon's personal life isn't any of your concern.

But it was. She wished him happiness, and he'd asked her to join Nelson's Tea. How could she agree to do so if she had no grasp of what Simon was going through?

There was also another thing to consider. Lucien had not survived his mission, and as yet, she had no explanation why. He'd never failed to avoid capture before. He'd been careful, taken precautions, which meant something or someone had foiled Lucien's plans. But who, other than Fouché or Barère, would do such a thing? How could she trust that someone within Simon's circle wasn't the culprit?

She had much to ponder before she agreed to help Simon continue his ruse de guerre. Perhaps that information could be gleaned by visiting Simon's house.

"It's been a very long day," she said, her nerves on edge. She doubted it would be easy to fool Goodayle. He seemed dogged in his determination to serve Simon. But if she wanted to leave Number Eleven and venture to Curzon Street without him knowing, she'd have to distract him.

She opened the door to her bedchamber. "If it isn't too much trouble, could you have a tub delivered to my room? In light of recent events, a bath by a warm fire would be positively divine."

Given a purpose, he straightened. "Of course. I'll have a tub brought up straightaway, as well as water heated for your use." His gentle smile gave no hint that he saw through her ruse. "In the meantime, if you need sustenance, I'll have Cook prepare something for you."

"Thank you. That would be most agreeable." She moved through the door. "Oh," she said, turning back to Goodayle as if suddenly remembering something of importance. "There is the matter of my maid—a Miss Cora Potts."

"Never fear, we have a maid here named Daisy who can see to your needs."

Of course they had a maid. "That is very kind." But Daisy did not fit into Gillian's plans. "I'm afraid you do not understand, Goodayle. Miss Potts traveled with me from Kent and is waiting for me to return to the Bull and Mouth Inn on Aldersgate Street. Do you know it?"

His brow cocked up. "I do."

"I could not possibly allow her to fear for my safety. Would it be too much to ask to arrange for her to join me here—tonight? I fear that after all we've been through the poor girl will worry herself sick if I do not return."

He bowed low. "I shall send for Miss Potts and your belongings without delay. You will have everything you need by morning, Baroness."

She frowned.

"Is there something else, my lady?" he asked.

"Well, you see, Miss Potts is unaccustomed to city life. Because of that, she does not trust easily, as I'm sure you understand. I daresay she will not accompany *any* servant." She behaved demurely for his benefit, batting her lashes and worrying her hands. "She has seen more than enough to know not to trust a stranger, and after . . . Well, I cannot bear to think—"

"I will retrieve her myself. You have my word."

She loathed her machinations. Goodayle seemed like a good man, but she had no choice. "Thank you, Goodayle," she said. She began to close the door to hide her triumphant smile.

He put his hand on the door to stop her, causing her momentary panic. "Forgive me, but you'll need this," he said, handing her the candlestick, "until we get your room fully prepared and a fire going in the hearth."

"Of course." Gillian nodded her thanks and took the candlestick from Goodayle's hand. "You have thought of everything, and I am indebted to you."

She closed the door to her bedchamber, leaned against it, and glanced about the poorly lit room, her mind made up. She was going to Curzon Street.

SIMON FROWNED AS the carriage jolted into motion. His desires, hopes, and dreams were nothing if not forfeit now that Gillian had walked back into his life. He'd tried to forget her, but now that he'd seen her, held her—even if at the expense of her broken heart—all he could think about were her soulful, beautiful, chocolate-brown eyes, and experiencing her painful loss as if it were his own.

Chauncey was dead. He was trying to accept it, but the process was exhausting, frustrating, and angering him beyond measure. There was no way to make this right. Only one thing would ease his tortured mind—sleep. But the comforts of a bed would not resolve the problems he faced. The baron had never been careless, never. How had Fouché's men caught up to him?

He laid his head back against the squabs and squeezed his eyes shut. His racing thoughts made his head ache. What would tomorrow bring? Gillian had helped them avert a grand plot of catastrophic proportions. If not for Chauncey's warning, England might have lost one of the greatest boons to its dwindling and brittle morale. The British people were tired of blockades and embargoes that prevented purchasing

French goods anywhere but on the black market.

He opened his eyes. What the people didn't understand was that this momentary peace was an illusion. Napoleon had amassed a fleet. Rebels were being slaughtered in France, Fouché's men had infiltrated England, and now Gillian was involved. Her involvement endangered her life, a matter that caused Simon grave concern. She had successfully bolstered their intelligence to save Vice-Admiral Nelson's life, a feat that forever put him in her debt. As long as they had Nelson at the helm of Nelson's Tea, they *would* succeed in protecting England's shores. But without the vice-admiral, they were doomed to fail.

Would Gillian join them? If she didn't, he wasn't sure how long he could keep her safe.

How long he pondered the things that plagued his mind, he couldn't be sure. The extended ride helped Simon sort through his thoughts whenever he needed to settle his nerves or put on a brave face for his wife. Her infirmity drained his spirits. His inability to locate a doctor capable of healing her had become his bane.

The carriage pulled to a stop at the back entrance of Number Seventeen Curzon Street, and Simon straightened his shoulders and resumed his stiff countenance.

His footman immediately appeared, bowed, folded down the step, and opened the carriage door. "My lord."

Simon nodded briefly before exiting the coach and heading to the threshold where Archer, his butler, waited patiently on the stoop.

"Thank you, Archer," he said, moving through the open door. Archer followed and moved up beside Simon. He gave the butler his cane and then took off his coat, top hat, and gloves, handing them over one at a time. "Is everything well with my wife?"

Archer's expression grew more serious than it was by nature. "She is the same, my lord."

Another stab of guilt pained Simon afresh.

"There is another matter, however," Archer said, tilting his head. "His Grace, the Duke of Throckmorton, was here."

"Here?" Rock usually sent a summons requesting Simon appear at Throckmorton Hall. It was unlike his brother to travel to Curzon Street unless Constance was coming to visit Edwina. But what did it matter? Archer had said *was here*, and Simon simply did not have the wherewithal to ponder Rock's behavior now.

"Yes, my lord. His Grace waited for you in the study for an hour before he left."

"And Lady Constance?" he asked, hoping he hadn't missed a chance to see his favorite niece. "Did she call on my wife?"

"She didn't accompany him, my lord."

"I see." Though he didn't. Already six-and-ten, his young niece yearned for Society at a time when Rock was refusing her opportunities. After his wife's death aboard the *Caddock*—and almost losing Constance to pirates, too—he strictly monitored Constance's comings and goings, making her entirely too sheltered. She had a penchant for making rash decisions as a result. Yet for all her childishness, Constance was Simon's joy. She was full of vigor, just as her mother had been—God rest her soul—which was probably why Rock shielded her so. But could Simon blame his brother? He wanted to protect Gillian the very same way.

Simon shook his head. Danburys certainly had their fair share of misfortunes.

"Would you like to take your brandy in the study, my lord?"

He blinked, then cut a glance at Archer. "Yes." He could

use a drink, but as he glanced up the staircase, the pull to see his wife was stronger. He quickly changed his mind. "On second thought, no. It has been a damned wretched night, and I must see my wife."

"Yes, my lord." Archer began to move down the hall but turned back. "I thought you should know His Grace was staring at her painting again."

Simon shrugged. "A deep, abiding love does not dim when lost, Archer."

Family obligations and memories in Number Seventeen seldom lured Rock away from Throckmorton Hall, in particular, to Simon's parlor with its Broadwood pianoforte and portrait of Lady Olivia. His sister-in-law had adored playing the instrument when she was alive. Now Constance had grown quite accomplished, and she'd come to play for Edwina. Music was one of the few joys his wife could still experience.

"Send a message to the duke that I will visit Throckmorton when I am able," Simon directed.

Archer nodded, bowed, and took his leave.

Simon climbed the stairs, loathing the path his and Edwina's lives had taken. They'd been dutiful pawns in their parents' quest to join two families. Making the most of their lives together, they'd become friends, trusted confidants, and lovers out of necessity. Edwina was all that was just and good; she had the purest of hearts. She didn't deserve the kind of pain and suffering she endured simply by trying to give him an heir.

Damn him to eternal hell. Edwina deserved more than he'd been able to provide. She deserved to be loved the way Rock had loved Lady Olivia, not to be the woman a man married when he could not have the lady he truly loved. Didn't every woman?

A warm light penetrated the hall as it spilled out from the door to Edwina's room, which was currently slightly ajar. He hesitated a moment, trying to control the internal battle waging between his emotions.

"That should be . . . my h-husband," Edwina said weakly. "Come . . . in, my l-lord." Her voice faltered whenever she strung too many words together.

Simon inhaled a breath to steady himself and then eased the door open. The all too familiar abhorrent aromas of laudanum, valerian root, and Peruvian bark entered his lungs. Nausea roiled in his stomach.

"My lady," he said, bowing. He paid no attention to the maid in the room as he moved quickly to his wife's side. He was accustomed to there always being one present.

Edwina was lying on a chaise longue, her body adorned in a delicate lace night rail, her hair brushed to a golden sheen, and her skin looking a shade too pale. "Come." Her dull blue eyes examined him as she stretched out her arm, but the limb dropped swiftly, as if the effort had been too great to maintain.

Her gentle smile, still capable of producing the single dimple in her cheek, took him back to the day they'd wed. She'd known then that he loved another, as had she. Their losses were deeply guarded secrets that only the two of them shared. They'd gone into their marriage with their eyes open, determined to make the best of their time together.

"T-Tell me. Did you . . . enjoy H-Holcroft's play?"

He bent down on one knee, lifted her hand to his lips, and kissed it gently, amazed once more by how thin Edwina's skin had now was, how fragile she had become. Her pulse throbbed faintly in her veins as she struggled to inhale a breath. They'd been down this road once before with Edwina coming close to death and then rebounding. He prayed it would be so again, though the doctors had given them little hope, citing everything from miasma, puerperal fever, consumption, and immobility as the causes.

"The theater," he said as he began to describe the night's events, as he always did upon his return, "was full." He used colorful language to bring the crowd and music and acting to life in her mind's eye. "People milled about in the latest styles. How I wish you could have seen it. There were feathers and frills, cravats, hats, and canes. The announcer dramatically directing the throng to be seated. The stage lights flared. The players began to sing—"

"Ah." Her eyes lit up from within. She inhaled a ragged breath. "And then a m-most . . . unexpected p-pause." Her voice was a raspy hiss.

"How did you know?" he asked, stunned.

"I was there." She smiled, confusing him all the more. "'S-Surprises . . . are all the r-rage at D-Drury, the th-theater of the age.'"

Simon blinked. Her poetic reference to the Theatre Royal was one he'd heard Gillian use before. But how could Edwina possibly know that? His blood ran cold. He didn't believe in coincidences.

"Surprises?" he broached.

She touched his cheek. "I know." Her weak caress forced him to remember the strong woman she used to be. She was the woman who'd encouraged him to leave the navy after he had wounded his leg, and hunt spies instead, and the wife who did not quibble about him being gone for months at a time while she struggled to bear a child, facing one disappointment after another.

"What is it you know?" he asked, his voice smooth but insistent as a chill settled in his core. "You must tell me, my lady."

"The t-time has come . . . I must t-tell you—" Edwina was struck by a fit of coughing.

Simon helped her sit up and move to her side. When the episode dissipated, he leaned her back and held a hand to her brow, fearing she'd worsened. She wasn't making sense. But her skin felt oddly cool to the touch, telling him there was no physical reason for her current state of mind.

"I kn-know about . . . Nelson," she finished.

How could she have possibly heard about the assassination attempt so fast? The servants were quick about gossiping amongst themselves, it was true, but there hadn't been enough time for the information to travel to Mayfair. Had there?

"Who told you?" he asked.

"Gillian."

His mouth went dry. She'd never spoken Gillian's name in his presence. They'd both agreed not to mention the names of their one true loves. "You cannot mean that the baroness was here?"

Wood crackled in the fireplace, and the logs fell. Startled, his reflexes on high alert, he spun around. "You may leave us," he told the maid.

The woman was dressed in an old, gray, wool gown and a white apron. Her hair was covered by a mop cap, and she nodded, curtsied, and scurried out the door.

Something oddly unsettling struck him about her. "Have we hired a new maid?"

"Do n-not be angry," she said, remorse contorting her features. "I w-wanted this."

His brow furrowed. "Wanted what?" He brushed an errant hair out of her face. "It has been a very long day. I fear my head must be muddled."

"She . . . is k-kind." Edwina paused to take a breath, the

sound jolting through him like a riptide. "I like her." Her voice cracked slightly. "She t-told me . . . you s-saved Nelson."

His jaw slackened. The new maid told her this? His heart sank in his chest. He turned and glanced at the door again, feeling the need to chase after the maid and prove Edwina wrong.

"She came." Edwina tried to rise. "I am—"

"Please, Edwina. You are overexciting yourself." He grabbed her shoulders and eased her back down on the pillows. "You must rest." She smiled wanly, and he continued, his voice soft. "I don't know how the baroness managed to get here, but she does me no favors. I wasn't the one who saved Admiral Nelson's life. She was."

She sucked in a pained breath. "I know." Her chest rose, and she turned her head as if in agony, writhing for a moment before relaxing once more. "I've a-always known . . . this day would c-come."

"What are you talking about?" As a rosy shade moved into her cheeks, he felt as if they were speaking about two different things. Years of pain, illness, and addiction had staked its claim on Edwina, ravaging her body with unrelenting force. "What did the baroness tell you?"

"She c-came to ask . . . m-my f-forgiveness," Edwina said, holding out her hand to him. He took it in his, feeling his vigor evaporate along with his innocent wife's. "But it was I who . . . needed absolution." She took a rattling breath. "Don't be angry. I s-stole . . . you from her."

"You're talking nonsense, Edwina." He shook his head, swallowing back the bile that had risen inside his stomach. Neither of them could change the past. If he could, he would wish her healthy. "None of that matters now."

"She is alone." She smiled, her eyes glimmering with affection. "Her husband is gone."

"But you are not. You never will be," he promised.

"You deserved b-better."

"Life isn't about what we deserve." How could he make her understand? "It's about what we do with the time we're given."

"Use it well," she said, nodding weakly. "I can g-go now. Happily s-so."

His eyes widened, and his breath caught. "What nonsense is this? You are not going anywhere. You cannot." He squeezed her hand, brought it to his lips, and tenderly kissed it. She didn't respond. His chest tightened, his heart stuck in his throat. "You need to rest so you can get well. You must. I demand it."

"No," she said, barely above a whisper as she stirred back from wherever lethargy had taken her. "You c-cannot stop . . . what has already b-begun. It's too late for me. B-But not . . . for you. You h-have my b-blessing." She licked her dry lips. "Kiss me . . . once m-more."

He pressed his mouth to hers and then pulled back a hairbreadth. "I will not allow you to go, Edwina. You cannot die. Do you hear me?" She didn't answer. "Fight!" he cried.

Footsteps padded down the hallway, but he ignored the people racing toward them.

"I am . . . at p-peace." She closed her eyes, a single tear trailing down her cheek. "Live, Simon. Go to her . . ." Her breath exhaled on a sigh.

"Edwina?" He laid his ear on her chest. Her heartbeat was faint, and then it stopped. "Edwina!"

War had forced him to reconcile with death, but not like this. Never like this!

"No . . ." He brushed her hair away from her face as servants gathered round them. He ignored them, straightening her gown and smoothing his hands down her arms.

They'd had so little time together during their marriage, and like a spring flower nurtured from bud to bloom, she was gone in the blink of an eye.

Eight

"And so he plays his part. The sixth age shifts
Into the lean and slippered pantaloon,
With spectacles on nose and pouch on side . . ."
~William Shakespeare, As You Like It

GILLIAN LEFT NUMBER Seventeen with tears streaming down her face. She hadn't meant to intrude or be discovered in Edwina's bedchamber. From the moment Goodayle had told her that Edwina was gravely ill, she'd been pulled to the woman by an invisible thread. She'd wanted to help Simon's wife in any shape or form, but when Edwina had asked for Gillian's forgiveness, then asked her to love Simon the way he was meant to be loved, she'd been so shocked, she'd lost all sense of time or place. And Simon had seen her. She was sure of it. Would he ever forgive her for the deceit?

Regardless, Gillian was glad to have spoken with the woman. Lady Danbury's quick wit had astonished her. They'd never met in person, but Lady Danbury had recognized Gillian almost immediately from her days onstage at Drury Lane. Not wanting to upset the poor woman, Gillian had admitted the truth of her identity. And for reasons she couldn't explain, Simon's wife had asked Gillian for forgiveness for not being strong enough to defy her parents and marry the man she loved, a man beneath her station, so that

Simon and Gillian could have been together, too. Gillian had assured Lady Danbury that she would have never known Lucien if that had happened, that she wouldn't be the woman she was today otherwise, and thanked her.

They'd embraced and cried, connected by loss and love. And now, after portraying Lady Fanny Nelson in public, Gillian understood the heavy burden Fanny carried by loving a man who loved another. Except in this instance, Gillian was the other woman.

Barely able to see past her tears, Gillian cut across Derby Street to Pitts Head Mews, meandering through Carrington Mews on her way to Number Eleven Bolton Street. She wiped her eyes and picked up her pace, walking more briskly to calm her frayed nerves and settle her racing thoughts. Dazed as she was, with her heart in her hand, she was wary enough to stay off Curzon's main thoroughfare where there was a greater risk of generating attention so late at night.

Lady Danbury didn't deserve the sickness that ravaged her body and soul. Emaciated and eager for news about Society, especially her husband's adventures, she had begged Gillian to reveal what she knew about Vice-Admiral Nelson's triumphant return. Had her husband looked sharp standing next to Nelson? Did the vice-admiral pay her husband the proper respect? It had felt entirely wrong passing along information about Simon and the vice-admiral, but she'd done so, frightening the poor woman against her better judgment. Eyes wide, Lady Danbury had listened to Gillian explain that Vice-Admiral Nelson had nearly been assassinated before her husband's eyes.

Gillian crossed her chest and prayed a silent prayer. Darting in and out of alcoves, she hugged her cloak more tightly around her as a carriage drew up alongside her. Horses' hooves clip-clopped on the thoroughfare, the beat out of time with her erratic heartbeat.

Another conveyance moaned past, its eerie creak exasperating her alarm. She gazed about frantically. Minute after minute, street after street, she walked. She'd meant well. Surely that made up for her lapse in good judgment by going to Simon's house.

A chill overtook her. She pulled the hood of her cloak higher, making sure the rough border dipped low enough to conceal the upper half of her face. Lady Danbury would surely tell Simon she'd been there, and in retaliation, he'd revoke his offer to join Nelson's Tea. Not becoming an intricate part of the organization and utilizing the skills Lucien had taught her would be a crime.

Besides, since Lucien had only gone by the name Corbet in France and had never used the name Chauncey in his dealings with the French, she had money, a title, and an established home. Though the grounds were now on Fouché's and Barère's map . . . Perhaps she could travel to the Cornish coast or farther north to Wales, out of Napoleon's reach?

But no, she couldn't run. She'd promised Lady Danbury that she would watch over Simon. Yet, if she stayed . . . well, she might be hunted down like a creature of the wood.

Oh, she was at sixes and sevens!

Lucien's words flooded her mind: *A fox outmaneuvered the hunter. Who better to lead a merry chase than a woman trying to save her own arse?*

Inhaling deeply, Gillian made up her mind. It would be better if she left early in the morning. A hunted woman was not what Simon or Nelson's Tea needed. She would pray Lady Danbury would forgive her, and then she would force herself to forget the man who made her heart beat with ruthless abandon.

Instantly sobered, Gillian left Shepherd Market and hastened toward Piccadilly, leaving White Horse Street behind.

Two men stepped out of an alcove and started walking behind her. Their laughter, an unwelcome distraction, wasn't what piqued her interest, but their French banter, which set her heart racing. Alarm rushed through her as she recalled the men she'd encountered from Box Four.

Desperate to make it to Number Eleven on Bolton Street and the safety she would find there, Gillian picked up her pace. But her quick actions weren't enough.

"You cannot outrun us, *petit rat*," one of them called after her.

Rats were problem solvers. They sensed danger and knew how to get out of tight spots. Gillian didn't mind the comparison. But if she intended to live out the night, she'd need to fight them on her own terms. She started to run, leading the men on a chase through a maze of buildings along Half Moon Street. She turned onto Clarges Street, but the footsteps sounded against the cobblestones behind her. She borrowed a stone wall for support and stopped to listen, easily gauging the distance between herself and her attackers. She would not be able to evade them. She needed to prepare for a counterattack.

Gillian moved into an alleyway, a dead end that would force the men to approach her and leave their backs unguarded. She pulled two sharp metal hairpins out of her coiffure and waited. The two men followed, blocking her exit, just as she suspected they would.

"You are trapped, *ma chérie*," the man who stood in the shadows said.

He pointed to his partner, who advanced. Gillian braced herself, spacing her feet wide and angling her right side toward the man in anticipation of his next move.

"If you do not rethink your intentions, this will not go well for you," she warned.

The first man said nothing but watched from afar like a

voyeur. The second one, however, bolted forward. He had no weapons that she could see. Apparently, he'd chosen to use brawn against her, perhaps desiring to snap her neck to prevent her from alerting passersby.

But she was ready. She counted his lumbering footsteps, one by one, judging his quickness of foot and body alignment, and calculating his weight and momentum. As he closed in, he raised his fists, aiming a blow to her face. She ducked what would have been a debilitating injury and stabbed one of the needlelike hairpins into the man's inner thigh. He He howled and bowed his back to grab his leg, and attacked again, lumbering toward her. Gillian dodged the man again.

In his momentary lapse, she flicked her cloak off her shoulders and over his head so he couldn't see. He struggled, his anger rising, as she stalked him, waiting for the precise moment he'd free his head. When he did, she sank the other hairpin into his neck.

Eyes wide with surprise, he grabbed her arm, taking her with him as he staggered backward. He cried out. She thought she'd heard him say, "Saint! Help!"

Gillian flicked her stare to the other man, prepared for the next round of attack. To her surprise, the other Frenchman simply backed away, retreating toward the street. She retrieved the dagger she kept strapped to her thigh as a last resort and followed, her elbows bent to guard her head and torso as she neared the street. But when she cleared the alley, her attacker's accomplice—and any knowledge of who he was—had simply vanished.

Gillian couldn't take the chance that he'd return, however, and took off at a run, darting past stately homes with wrought iron fences as she wove her way through Mayfair to ensure she wasn't followed. Shaken and exhausted, she walked slowly to Bolton Street and Number Eleven. There, she stepped onto the stoop, glanced around to see if anyone was watching her, and then pulled several more hairpins out of her tussled hair to pick the lock.

Click. The mechanism disengaged. She opened the door and quickly slipped inside. The house was eerily quiet, though she'd hadn't spent a night within yet so she couldn't be sure what to expect. She made her way past the longcase clock toward the stairs. Halfway there, she heard a man's voice.

"Did you find what you were looking for, Baroness?"

Goodayle's question startled her, but she managed not to jump. "Yes." Turmoil burned inside her, and she straightened her skirts and patted her hair, trying to appear calmer than she felt. "Were you able to locate my maid, Goodayle? I'm at a loss without her."

"Of course." He stepped into the open, emerging from a dark corner near the longcase clock. "Miss Potts will be ready to attend you in the morning."

"Wonderful," she said, glad that something was finally going her way. "Thank you, Goodayle. Now, if you'll excuse me, I shall retire for the night. It's been an eventful day."

"I can see that, Baroness." He cocked his brow. "Pardon me for saying so, my lady, but I notice you did not return with your cloak."

"My cloak?" She placed her hand on the banister and stopped midstep. *Clever man!* Goodayle had seen her sneak out of the townhouse. "It's of no use to me now," she said truthfully. The garment had served its purpose.

Her comment seemed to take Goodayle aback. "Shall I send Daisy up to assist you? She has a knack with unruly stains."

She glanced down at herself once more, noting the blood that splattered all over her clothing. *Botheration!* She had borrowed Daisy's clothes and had been in such a hurry to make it back to Bolton Street that she hadn't considered the way she looked or how she was going to explain the bloodstains. "Extend my apologies to Daisy. I will replace her uniform before I leave."

He nodded stiffly. "Have you . . . decided to refuse Lord Danbury's offer, then?"

After she'd snuck into Simon's home and spoken to his ailing wife, Simon would never forgive her. "My decision," she said on a sigh, "is complicated."

"Most decisions are," he said, his eyes gleaming in the half-light. "Be advised. In the future, if you need anything, Baroness, anything at all, you have only to ask and it will be done."

"Thank you, Goodayle." She managed a smile, genuinely grateful she'd found sanctuary in London, a place where Fouché's and Barère's men couldn't reach her until she could figure out where to go next. "I shall retire, then, and gladly so."

"As you wish, Baroness." He walked to a hallway table and grabbed the lone candlestick there. Its flaming wick dimmed, then flared, then barely flickered as he moved across the marble foyer and handed it to her. She accepted the cold unyielding pewter, wrapping her fingers around the looped handle, relieved that the man's questions had come to a halt.

Goodayle bowed, and without saying another word, he turned, leaving her to her own devices.

She quivered. That terrifying ordeal was over, wasn't it? Except . . .

Good hounds never lost the scent.

Her hands began to shake. She tightened her grasp on the bannister, prickles of unease crawling down her spine. Had the men in the alley stolen her resilience? No. She'd risen from squalor and joined forces with a spy. Lucien had taught her never to turn away from a challenge. She was made of sterner stuff.

With Goodayle's footsteps a distant tap on the marble,

Gillian climbed the staircase, moving slowly past the exquisite gilded landscapes—more lush and vibrant in the candlelight—and then by the pairs of unseeing canvas eyes that led to the next floor. The glow from her candle cast eerie shadows in the hallway as she came to stand before her bedchamber door.

I am safe, she told herself. But Lucien was not. Lady Danbury was not. There would be no rejoicing this night. Nor any other for that matter.

She opened the door, a moment's panic seizing her chest as her gaze fell on the copper tub near the fireplace. A washstand had been placed nearby, and she was eager to remove her garments, stained as they were with a stranger's blood—a man she'd killed. In some small measure, she was glad that Goodayle had seen her leave Number Eleven. Is that how he had known to wait to prepare her bath?

Gillian moved into the room, closed the door behind her, and set down the candle on a bedside table. The room was dark with only the sparse candlelight and the fire snapping and crackling in the hearth. She stretched her aching body, feeling as if she carried the world on her shoulders. And she had for much too long.

Her emotions rose to the surface. Here, in the privacy of her room, a tear trailed down her cheek. Despising the weakness, she swiped it angrily away with the back of her hand and began stepping out of her disguise, piece by practical piece—her bloodstained apron, the leather bracings that held her knives over her stockings, her stays and the sheath she hid there, and finally, her shift. She gazed at the bed where she'd laid weapon after weapon—short blade here, and small pistol there—feeling the weight on her conscience lighten.

Why hadn't Lucien allowed her to accompany him to France? If she had been with him, then perhaps . . .

Another tear fell. She could not change the past.

Devil's hounds! I will not cry again.

She'd fought too hard and come too far to lose control of herself now. If only she had someone to talk to, someone to whom she could confide her fears. But Lucien was gone, and she had yet to see Cora. At this hour, Gillian guessed her maid would most likely be abed.

She stretched again, this time arching her tired arms over her head. Her muscles complained as she moved to the copper tub. She moaned with delight as she dipped her toe in the water. It was still warm—more evidence of Goodayle's uncanny timing.

Gillian stepped into the tub and slipped beneath the surface, releasing an audible sigh. She submerged her body, cleansing away her sorrow, guilt, and pain. Then she sank down, allowing the water to wash over her face. Beneath the surface, she held her breath, envisioning her garden, her home, and the solitude and sanctuary she and Lucien had experienced there, hanging on to the life they'd once lived. But she couldn't. Her lungs squeezed. Her pulse began to pound like a death knell, every inch of her screaming for air. It was useless to cling to the past. She could never get back what she'd lost.

Lucien was dead.

She broke through the surface of the water and inhaled a wrenching breath. She smoothed the hair away from her face and settled her head back against the rim of the tub. Relaxing there, she fought to bring her heartbeat back under control and closed her eyes.

The scent of leather and spice infiltrated her senses. Was this still part of her imaginings? Had she finally come so unhinged that she could actually smell Simon when he wasn't there? It was impossible for him to be. She'd left him in his townhouse with his wife. And yet, Gillian fought an odd sensation that he was there, that she was being watched.

A strange fizzling sound fractured the stillness, and Gillian sprang to attention. She reached for one of her knives, sloshing water over the sides of the tub. The weapon securely in hand, she surveyed the room, stifling the urge to scream. When would this night, and the dangers it brought, ever end?

In the corner of the room, she spied a small flame blaze in the darkness, then disappear. Tobacco filled the room as another glowing ember took shape. Someone *was* in her room!

"Forgive my intrusion," a familiar voice said.

It *was* Simon!

She scrambled for something to cover herself even as an unbidden heat coiled in her belly. "How did you get in here?" she blurted, scarcely recognizing her own voice.

Had he entered while she'd been underwater? Or had he somehow left his wife after discovering she'd been there and come for retribution? Thinking upon it, she supposed the latter was possible since she'd been forced to fight for her life in the alley. She had no earthly idea how much time had passed since she'd last seen him.

He studied her thoughtfully. "I snuck in . . . The same way you entered my wife's bedchamber." There was an underlying sadness in his voice she'd only heard once before: the day they'd said goodbye five years earlier. Something was terribly wrong.

"I meant no harm," she quickly told him. "Goodayle said your wife was ill, and I—"

"Didn't believe him?" Simon stood up from the chair he was sitting in and slowly limped forward, his six-foot height looking impressive in the candlelight. His brown hair was abnormally mussed, his cravat askew. And he was still the handsomest man she'd ever known. "Edwina told me why you'd come. I thought you should know—and there is no gentle way to tell you this—she died shortly after that."

She gasped, stricken by sadness for Simon and his wife but also riddled with guilt. Dear God, *was* Lady Danbury's death her fault? Tears welled in her eyes. "Oh, Simon! I'm so very sorry. I never meant to cause your wife any harm. I learned of the old medicinal remedies in Kent, ways to help the sick, and I thought . . ."

"You thought what?" he asked, his tone solemn.

"I thought I could help. I wanted to help her get well. But I did not comprehend how ill she was. And she . . . she . . ." Gillian couldn't finish. How could she reveal that Lady Danbury had pleaded for Gillian to vow to always stay by Simon's side? This was neither the time nor place for such an admission. Besides, she wasn't sure she ever wanted Simon to know.

"She told me she'd asked you for forgiveness," he said. The tip of his spicy-scented cigar blazed red as he took another excruciatingly long puff. His emotions were unreadable, but she suspected he meant to hide them.

"And I sought hers, as well." Her voice broke as her heavy heart sank into her belly. The bathwater suddenly felt entirely too cold, and she began to shiver. "I'm truly sorry for your loss, Simon. Lady Danbury was kind. I—"

"Will listen to what I have to say," he cut in.

She startled. What could he possibly say to her now that she hadn't already told herself? "Of course," she relented, sliding down in the tub to hide her body from his piercing stare. "I understand."

"Do you?" He walked forward until he was standing before her. She clung to the wet towel she'd draped over herself in her embarrassment. "You are an educated woman with ideals and fascinating talents, but you are wrong about many things, Gillian."

"Apparently, too many to count." She bit her lip in dismay. Where was he going with this conversation? She wasn't sure she wanted to know. One accusatory word from him after all that had occurred and her heart might never recover.

Simon shoved his hand through his hair. "My wife—God rest her soul—was an uncomplicated creature. She was genuine and loyal, dutiful and kind, as you generously pointed out." He puffed on his cigar, glanced at the fire, and then moved toward it to throw the stub into the flames.

"She was in love once, as we were," he said, looking her direction. The word *once* fractured Gillian's heart. "But her parents thought the man she wanted to marry only desired Edwina for her money. Unfortunately, that may have been the case. Her parents, the Landon-Fitzhughs, caught the man attempting to whisk Edwina off to Gretna Green in the middle of the night to be married. Desperate to save their daughter's reputation, they turned to my father. A contract was made up that would impact my social status and naval career."

She nodded slowly to show him she was listening, though the pain she saw in his eyes made her yearn to throw her arms around him and hold him.

"Sir Landon-Fitzhugh had connections within the Admiralty, you see. After I was injured aboard HMS *Captain*, my father, a powerful man I dutifully strove to impress, worried about my future. I was informed about Edwina's situation and asked to step in honorably to save her reputation. It would be a career move, as well, assuring me a place in politics. I had no interest in government at the time. My loyalties lay elsewhere with Admiral Nelson."

He stopped to stare at the fire. "I sought the admiral's help, knowing he would give me the best advice. He said the connections I could make within the Admiralty would allow access to information he could not readily get, reminding me of the countless times he'd asked for more frigates, only to be ignored. Shortly afterward, I agreed to the contract. I was bound to honor that contract when I met you, as much as I wished otherwise." He began to pace the carpet before the hearth. "Edwina was devastated by her lover's desertion, and I—loving you as I did—stood by to watch you marry someone else."

She'd been so caught up in the whirlwind that had been her wedding day—cursing Simon's indifference—that she'd neglected to consider how her marriage had affected him. All this time, she had believed he'd never loved her. How could a man love a woman he so easily cast aside? But she'd been wrong. She raised up in the tub, desiring to comfort him, not knowing if she could bear any more.

Firelight highlighted his body as he turned back toward the hearth and borrowed the mantel for support. His voice was thick and unsteady as he continued pouring out his soul to her. "Edwina and I married unified in the hope that we could make the best of our situation. We never spoke of our heartbreaking losses again."

So it had all been an illusion. Simon had been wearing an iron mask. That revelation shattered the last of the walls surrounding her heart.

His voice was uncompromising but surprisingly gentle as he added, "Edwina is gone now. She told me she was grateful you came to her." He cleared his throat and turned to face her. "She likes—liked—you. And as she drew her last breath, she made me promise never to let you go."

He left the fireplace, limped toward her, and knelt down before the tub. "As she requested, I have come to you, Gillian. I am here, body and soul. I am now at liberty to ask for your pardon. Could you ever forgive me?"

His entreaty combined with his nearness stirred her senses to dizzying new heights. "There is nothing to forgive, Simon." In truth, there wasn't. She'd yearned to hear him apologize for his deceit but knew she was as much to blame for their past as he was.

"Truly?" His unrelenting gaze searched hers. "I cannot bear the thought of your derision."

Her heart hitched. She wasn't the doe-eyed girl Simon had met at Drury Lane. She was a seasoned woman, a widow mourning those who were no longer parts of their lives: Lucien and even Simon's wife. But his apology, no matter how long she'd yearned for it, was too much, too soon. "I have learned that channeling my energy where it can be most effective can help me accept what I cannot change. Life is too short to harbor ill will."

He shook his head. "Time has been good to you, Gillian," he said, his voice a silken caress, if not sorrowful in its delivery.

She trembled, resisting her desire to touch him. "To you, as well."

She shrank back in the tub, feeling awkward and embarrassed again, as her emotions swirled inside her—fear of herself and what she might do in light of the sadness that settled over them like a shroud. Concern for what their confessions might bring, as the threshold they just crossed tore at the fragile boundary between them.

"You are tired," he said. "How long has it been since you have slept?"

She'd forgotten. How long had it been? She'd only been able to doze off and on while traveling from Kent. "Forty-eight hours, perhaps?"

He leaned forward, his arm brushing against hers as he reached for a cloth and a bar of soap.

"What are you doing?" she asked, suddenly apprehensive. She watched him lather the cloth. Did he actually mean to bathe her like a child? Torment began to gnaw at her belly. And yet, her body refused to move.

"I used to bathe Edwina like this." He was so close, his

breath sent tendrils of fire racing through her veins as he began to stroke her shoulders. "I cannot lose you again, Gillian."

"Simon." Her heart turned over in her chest, and she gazed into his eyes. Emotions she'd held in check burst forth, and she unleashed her misery, sobbing out her despair with abandon. Life was unfair! Lucien and Lady Danbury were dead; several men had tried to kill her. And now the pain she'd tried so hard to bury had been yanked to the surface.

Simon knew these things, too, and he drew her close, allowing her time to expend her sorrow as he traced an imaginary path across her back, comforting her in ways only he could. When at last her tears were spent, he guided her to her feet and wrapped a dry towel around her. Then with gentle ease, he lifted her into his arms and carried her to the bed.

"Simon, no," she rushed out on a gasp.

He couldn't possibly mean to—

"Shh," he cooed. "If I don't get you into bed, you will catch a chill. The water has grown cold."

He laid her down gently, as if she were a babe, and pulled the sheets over her body. When the counterpane was tucked around her, he reached for her hand, interlocking their fingers. "You are more beautiful than I ever imagined anyone could be."

"Don't say that, Simon," she said. "I am many things but not beautiful. I am weak, addle-headed, and a heartless wanton because I am not running as far away from you as I can."

"You are wrong. You are the most beautiful woman I've ever seen." He let go of her hand and placed it beneath the covers. "I will not ask you how blood got splattered on your clothes. I have seen with my own eyes that it isn't yours, and that is all that matters. Sleep now. You are safe. We will be at it again in the morning, hammer and tongs."

"We?" she asked, unable to snuff out the hope that filled her breast.

His stare raked boldly over her, heating her blood. "I like the sound of that, though the cost weighs heavily on my soul."

Gillian smiled. "Mine too." She closed her eyes, but she knew sleep wouldn't easily come. One question still plagued her mind: what would tomorrow bring?

Nine

"His youthful hose, well saved a world too wide
For his shrunk shank, and his manly voice,
Turning again toward childish treble, pipes . . ."
~William Shakespeare, As You Like It

HOURS AFTER HE'D left Gillian's room and the hackney driver had delivered him home, Simon sank into a leather chair in his study at Number Seventeen Curzon Street. The weight of the world settled on his shoulders as he contemplated the somber quiet that filled the townhouse. He was accustomed to schedules and unsettled by the thought that there would be no more doctors coming and going at all hours. He took a generous sip from his second tumbler of brandy. At this point in his life, he cared not a whit what condition Archer found him in when the sun rose through the study windows and his butler entered through the large oak doors.

Surrounded by a menagerie of bookcases, journals, and maps, Simon was at a loss. He didn't know where to begin. It was his duty, however, to take the situation in hand. The Landon-Fitzhughs were on sabbatical in Bath, where Sir Landon-Fitzhugh partook in the medicinal waters. It fell to Simon to inform them of their daughter's death, and it was information that needed to be delivered with care via a courier. A carriage also needed to be sent to retrieve them in their bereavement.

Until the Landon-Fitzhughs arrived, funeral rites would be discharged and Edwina's body prepared for burial, a matter that needed to be taken care of without delay. At most, a body lasted two weeks before decay set in, depending on the weather, except for those who'd endured lengthy illnesses or addictions of some kind. At least that's what he'd been told. And that meant Edwina's body would need to be laid to rest as soon as possible. His course of action would also be determined by Edwina's parents, of course. He knew they would want to bury their only daughter in the family crypt on their country estate, but Edwina's relationship with her family had suffered greatly after she and Simon had wed. Her parents had never quite forgiven her disobedience and nearly tarnishing their good name.

Simon leaned back, resting his head on the tall chairback. Edwina had been particularly fond of Chelsea, and in particular St. Luke's Cemetery where Sir Thomas More, Lady Jane Cavendish Cheyne, and Sir Hans Sloane were interred. "Holy ground," she'd called it.

Devil take it, to hell with what the Landon-Fitzhughs desired. He'd write a letter to Mr. Crofton, the vicar at St. Luke's, and make arrangements for his wife to join the likes of great men and women who'd found their heavenly reward. It would be a sensible gesture to have Chauncey's body collected from Kent and delivered to St. Luke's, as well, though he would have to get Gillian's approval first.

His mind made up, Simon opened his lap desk, set a piece of parchment on the writing slope, and picked up a quill. He thoughtfully crafted a letter to the Landon-Fitzhughs, considering the shock and their emotional state as he wrote, then sprinkled sand over the script and folded the missive. When that was done, he took off his signet ring and pressed his family crest into the foolscap, sealing the note in wax before putting it aside. He'd have Archer arrange for his correspondence to be transported to Bath via one of his coachmen.

The preoccupation of his mind and courtesy to Edwina's relatives in place, he turned his attention to his second order of business—one crucial to Britain's political climate. Instructions would need to be sent to the men he'd enlisted to join Nelson's Tea so they could be introduced to Vice-Admiral Nelson, learn what was expected of them, and discover what their first mission would entail.

It had taken Simon a year to locate and recruit the most trusted and capable men he could find. And now, with the attempt on Vice-Admiral Nelson's life, Philippe d'Auvergne's work with *émigrés* in Jersey and his forgery of French assignat notes at thirty thousand pounds a year in jeopardy, and the added loss of Chauncey, they could not risk waiting to put their men into the field. Obtaining genuine intelligence took time, and time was of the essence. The United Irishmen and the Corresponding Societies plotted to topple the monarchy. Henry Dundas claimed there was also something else afoot inside the War Office, shifting alliances that endangered England's shores.

With so much at stake, the Marquess of Stanton would need to be contacted first. Stanton would handle the arrangements, taking Vice-Admiral Nelson's and Hendry Dundas's schedules into consideration. Goodayle would prepare the servants and the town house at Number Eleven for twenty-one people, not including Simon. And Gillian, if she agreed to join Nelson's Tea, would act as hostess.

Once the men were assembled, the organization would stretch its arms across Scotland, Wales, England, and Cornwall, to France and Spain. In addition to the twenty-one members of the group, there were others who would work behind the scenes to ensure the operation was a success abroad, such as d'Auvergne—already in place and working for the Admiralty—and Don Alberto Ramon Vasquez in San Sebastian, and Filbert Seaton, the Earl of Pendrim, in Cornwall. The two men were old acquaintances and free traders capable of smuggling men and supplies between England and Spain. The connections were vital to their success.

Keeping track of the group would be a challenging endeavor, however, a distraction Simon needed, especially now. Some at the Admiralty claimed their objective was impossible, but Simon meant to prove the naysayers wrong. He had the former war secretary's approval, and King George III's, the Prince of Wales's, and Nelson's support. All he needed now was for Gillian to agree to join their cause.

She'd proven her loyalty by fighting alongside her husband until the bitter end. She'd even been able to neutralize Chauncey's assassin, successfully warn Nelson, and defend herself from her attacker at the theater. He also suspected she'd had another encounter with the enemy on her way home from his townhouse. The blood on her disguise hinted as much. Nelson's Tea could use a woman of her caliber, a female spy capable of infiltrating the upper crust. He prayed she'd join him in the endeavor, that she wouldn't allow their past to cloud her decision.

He put down the quill and wrapped his hand around his tumbler before draining his brandy once again.

Gillian wasn't the woman he'd once loved. She was better, stronger, more enticing now than she'd ever been. The scars Simon had seen on her body—her shoulder blade, left hip, right knee, and ankle—indicated that the life Chauncey had trained her for had been a perilous one. Simon had been forced to grit his teeth when he'd helped her out of the tub and seen evidence of her previous wounds, just to keep from asking her about them. He was the one who'd arranged for her to marry the baron to keep her safe, not put her in danger.

Guilt unlike any he'd ever known assailed him. He blamed himself for Edwina's illness and her descent into addiction, as well as Gillian's widowhood. If he hadn't allowed Edwina to keep trying to give him a child, if the doctors he'd hired had been able to determine what ailed her and hadn't provided the laudanum she'd become addicted to, and if he'd never sent Chauncey to France, perhaps Edwina would still be alive and Gillian wouldn't be a widow. But he *had* done those things. *He* was responsible.

He pressed his lips together, choking back the fury that made his pulse race. There was nothing he could do to turn back time. Not one blasted thing. The cards had been dealt, and war was an art that knew no master.

Simon picked up his quill again and twirled it between his fingers. He dipped the hollow shaft of the molted feather into an inkwell and began writing the first sentence of many dispatches he'd be sending throughout the day. No matter the personal tragedies any of them faced, they could not falter.

GILLIAN AWOKE AND wiped the sleep from her eyes as a knock sounded on the door.

"Enter," she said, shifting on the pillows.

The door slowly opened and her maid, Cora, appeared. In her hands, she carried a tray of food. She curtsied, walked toward Gillian, and lowered the tray to the nightstand. "Good mornin', m'lady."

Gillian smiled, pleased to see that Cora had been safely delivered to the townhouse, just as Goodayle had said. "Good morning, Cora. You had no trouble arriving here, I hope?"

"No trouble a'tall." Cora turned back to the door and closed it. She scurried to Gillian's bedside and made a good show of plumping the pillows behind Gillian's back so she could sit up more comfortably. "I am so 'appy to see ye again, m'lady. When ye didn't return to the Bull and Mouth, I was beside meself. Thought ye'd been killed, I did."

She moved to the windows and busied herself opening the heavy drapes to allow decadent rays of rare London sunshine into the room. "Brought ye up a tray. I figured ye'd be 'ungry since ye're normally up afore dawn."

"Thank you, Cora." Her maid was right. Oversleeping wasn't her normal routine, but her life had changed drastically and this wasn't her room. The bed, nightstand, wardrobe, sideboard with wash basin, and bric-a-brac on the mantel weren't hers, though she appreciated the almost imperceptible door cloaked by wallpaper beside the fireplace, which offered a quick escape should the need arise.

Sorrow filled her as images of the past several days flooded her mind. Lucien. The theater. Simon. The assassins.

Remnants of Simon's spicy cigar lingered in the air. The copper tub still sat before the fire. She was safe, cared for. Simon had stepped in to help her. When all appeared lost, he had a tendency to swoop in like an avenging angel to calm her spirits and usher her through the darkest turmoil. "Life always finds a way," she said softly.

"What's that ye say, Baroness?" Cora began to tidy up the room. She picked up the maid's uniform Gillian had worn the night before and looked at her, bewildered. "Please tell me this isn't yer blood!"

"It isn't," she said truthfully, then gave a dismissive wave of her hand. "Oh, I am famished. What have you brought me to eat?" she asked quickly.

"No, ye don't. Ye'll not be changin' the subject on me." Cora examined the uniform more closely. "A neck wound, I wager, by the angle of the stain. Tell me that ye didn't 'ave a run-in with more assassins," she said, her voice quivering.

Cora had been working for Gillian for too long; the woman could always see past Gillian's facades.

Gillian climbed out of bed and stepped behind the screen, using the privacy to allow herself more time to think. She had much to ponder: what to tell Cora, whether or not she'd stay and join Nelson's Tea, her feelings for Simon. When she appeared moments later, Cora was standing there waiting, her arms crossed over her chest. She'd already straightened the sheets, plumped Gillian's pillows again, and placed the breakfast tray on the bed.

"Do ye intend to tell me what 'appened or not?"

"I scared you, and for that, I am sorry. It couldn't be helped." Gillian moved to the washbasin to cleanse her hands.

Cora harrumphed. "It will take more than a colossal stranger callin' in the dead of night and takin' me to a place I've never been to scare me, Baroness."

That much was true. One of Cora's responsibilities was to dress Gillian's wounds when the situation called for it. "The man you speak of is Goodayle. He's Lord Danbury's butler."

"Lord Danbury!" Cora's mouth formed an O, but she covered it quickly with her hand. "Is this 'is townhouse?"

"Shh." She waved her hands to calm Cora down. "It is, and I haven't quite decided what I think about that yet." She sat back down on the bed and lifted the platter cover. Cora had brought her plum cake, eggs, and ham. There was also a pitcher of tea and chocolate. "How divine," she said on a sigh. When had she last eaten? She couldn't be sure. "Thank you, Cora. You take such great care of me."

Cora beamed proudly. "'Tis me job, m'lady. Ye tend to think of everyone else but yerself. 'Igh time that changes, I say." She rushed forward and pointed to the tray. "And look! Someone slipped ye a note! Who do ye think it's from?"

"Lord Danbury," she said. "I recognize his handwriting. Only he and his staff know that I am here."

"Well, go on, open it," Cora insisted. "Whatever it is, it must be important."

Gillian nodded. She popped the red wax seal and opened the missive, folding back the foolscap edges and revealing the perfectly formed script. She read the note, then dropped it in her lap. It was an invitation.

"Well?" Cora asked, crossing her arms and tapping her foot. "What does it say?"

She locked eyes with Cora. "There's to be a meeting here tonight. Lord Danbury requests my presence."

"What kind of meetin'?"

Gillian's blood stirred. "The kind involving secrecy." She clamped the missive in her lap as butterfly wings fluttered to life inside her. Simon had been true to his word: he meant to include her in Nelson's Tea. This was her chance to honor Lucien, to continue his work.

"Is it wise to continue this way of life, Baroness?" Cora asked, as if reading her mind. "Assassins 'ave come after ye on numerous occasions, and ye've barely escaped. Ye do not 'ave nine lives."

"Of course I don't. I am not a feline." She cut a glance at the widow's garb behind Cora. The gown was draped over the back of an overstuffed chair by the hearth. Its very presence forewarned what lay ahead. Men lived and died serving the crown. But she was determined to do what Lucien had trained her to do, to give her life meaning. "I must be honest with myself. I have been given a taste of danger, and it is in my blood now. What else am I to do, Cora?" she asked. "You know how much I enjoyed working alongside my husband."

"The baron would likely want ye to continue to fight in 'is rebellion, but at a safe distance." Cora took Gillian's hand in hers. "But 'e is gone. We cannot go back to Kent. Not after—"

"I know." She nodded. "Lord Danbury is forming a clandestine organization that Admiral Nelson intends to use against Napoleon, Fouché, and Barère."

"Admiral Nelson?" Cora smiled broadly. "The very same 'oo won the battle of Copenhagen?"

At Gillian's nod, Cora left Gillian and crossed the room. She picked up the bloody apron. "I cannot tell ye what to do, m'lady, but one way to 'onor yer 'usband's memory would be to carry on 'is good work. The people of France be sufferin'. We've seen it."

Gillian chuckled. "Lord Danbury used the same argument with me." She smiled at Cora fondly. "The baron would approve of your wise counsel."

"It isn't 'is approval I seek, m'lady." She dropped the apron. She approached the copper tub and dragged her finger around its lip on her way to the fireplace. "Be there another reason ye doubt yer decision?" she asked over her shoulder as she dropped to bank the fire.

"I'm not sure," Gillian lied. She paused a beat, then gave in. Cora would figure it out sooner or later. The woman had a knack for deducing Gillian's thoughts. "Yes. There is . . . As you said, it isn't safe in Kent. If I don't agree to help Lord Danbury, I shall have to move far away."

Cora glanced over her shoulder. "What are ye not tellin' me?"

"You wouldn't approve."

Her maid rose to her feet with a hot poker in her hand. "What 'arm could there be in not attendin' the meetin'?"

"As you know, Lord Danbury meant something to me once."

"And?" Cora asked. "Are ye afraid yer affection for the gentleman will be rekindled?"

It already had. "I went to visit Lady Danbury last night."

"Whatever for?"

"She was dying, Cora," Gillian said, her voice breaking, as Cora dropped the poker and rushed to her side. "When Goodayle told me Lady Danbury was sick, I was beside myself with worry. I've never wished her ill. I thought . . . I thought to help her, you see."

"And did ye?" Cora asked, sitting on the bed beside Gillian.

She shook her head. "Goodayle failed to mention how badly the lady's health had declined. My heart ached when I saw her. She was incredibly thin, pale, and near death." She shivered uncontrollably. Cora laid something warm about her shoulders as Gillian explained the state in which she'd found Lady Danbury, the smell of saffron and laudanum that permeated the woman's room, and the conversation she had with Simon's wife. Gillian even told Cora that she was almost killed while returning to the townhouse and shared that Simon had come to her room.

"So, you see, it will be impossible to join Nelson's Tea and be impartial to Lord Danbury, especially after his wife made me promise to take care of him."

"Oh dear," she said. "And did she die?" Shock registered on Cora's face as Gillian nodded. "Poor man. But yer choice should be easy now. Ye loved 'im once." Cora inclined her head. "Is it possible ye love 'im still?"

"It's too soon to say." Indeed, the odds couldn't be more against them. She'd lost her husband violently, and Simon had just lost his wife to a lengthy illness. What would people say?

"Then ye owe it to yerself to stay and find out. After all, ye promised the lord's wife."

Gillian could always count on Cora to speak plainly and get to the heart of a matter. Lucien had hired her, and she'd been invaluable to Gillian since she'd come to work for her in Kent. She was tight-lipped, trustworthy, and reliable, qualities one did not always find in a servant. But Cora had become more than that. She was Gillian's confidant and friend. Her advice had never faltered before.

"Very well. I'll stay . . . for now."

She speared another piece of plum cake with her fork and sighed. She wasn't certain she could live so close to the man she'd loved and lost without forgetting her place. And could she openly hide her love and affection from the rest of the world, in keeping with her role as a widowed baroness?

"'Take thy seat of actors first,'" she quoted *Jubilee* aloud. "For such thy art, thou seem'dst as thou wert born for the stage only—yet thy manners such, thy probity so great, thou seem'dst unfit to have been there—" She stopped, unable to continue.

"I wish I could 'ave seen ye on the stage, Baroness. Ye must 'ave earned great praise." Cora disappeared behind a door and returned with a freshly pressed black gown devoid of frills. She laid it on the corner of the bed and put her hands on her hips. "What made ye think of that particular passage?"

The fork clattered to Gillian's plate as she put her hand on her chest. "It seemed appropriate somehow. What we do henceforth will force us to hide who we truly are."

Ten

"And whistles in his sound. Last scene of all,
That ends this strange eventful history..."
~William Shakespeare, As You Like It

SEVERAL DAYS LATER, Simon and many of the men he'd selected to join Nelson's Tea waited in his library for the meeting when the door to the library opened. "The Honorable Henry Dundas, former Secretary of State and War Secretary," Goodayle announced.

Dundas moved into the room and bowed to the group gathered there. "Good evening, Danbury," he said with a lilting Scottish accent.

"Dundas," Simon said, bowing his head. "Welcome."

Dundas, a well-known curmudgeon who left his position at the War Office in May after Prime Minister William Pitt's resignation, gave Simon a nod and then moved away, carrying a ledger and grumbling something about timetables as he walked over to Simon's desk. There, he sat down, turned to a specific page in said ledger, and picked up a quill to jot something within it.

"The Most Noble Lord Horatio Nelson, Viscount and Baron Nelson, Knight of the Bath, Vice-Admiral of the Blue, Duke of Brontë."

Staccato footsteps clicked against the marble floor of the

foyer as Vice-Admiral Horatio Nelson entered the library. He came to an abrupt halt as the entire assembly rose to greet him. Nelson rose to his full five-foot-seven-inch height. He reached up and removed his hat, turned, and offered it to Goodayle, who grasped the bicorn like a prized piece of porcelain. "Thank you, Goodayle, for that magnificent introduction."

Goodayle maintained his poise in the presence of his old commander and backed respectably out of the room.

A feast to the eyes, Nelson was dressed in military blue, his buttons shining a brilliant gold. His right sleeve was pinned conspicuously as he had no arm to fill it. He wore polished black pumps and formfitting white stockings. Dark circles shadowed his eyes, and he appeared drawn and tense, the effects of another bout of malaria having taken its toll, it seemed. His military bearing—posture, enthusiasm, and confidence—had been strictly enforced by his uncle throughout his career, evident by his firm constitution, the set of his brow, and the smile that didn't quite reach the eyes, affirming he'd seen and done things no man should.

Nelson stood stiffly in all his glory as he spotted Simon, clicked his heels, nodded, and then bowed a greeting. "Lord Danbury."

"Lord Nelson," Simon said, bowing in return. "Welcome to Number Eleven Bolton Street."

The awe the vice-admiral inspired was a rallying cry among the British people. For men of action, living a dual existence was no real hardship. One did what one had to do. But how did Nelson manage? He was married to a woman who would not give him a divorce. He flaunted a mistress before his wife, the Admiralty, and the *ton*, caring not a whit for public speculation and nearly making himself look ridiculous. And yet, Nelson held the hopes and dreams of the countless wives and children of the men who followed him.

Even now, Simon struggled to retain his height under the weight of twenty lives perched on his lapels. Nelson stood proudly, having balanced far more his entire life. He'd come to meet each and every man Simon had recruited, measuring them for muster, and the vice-admiral's approval was paramount to their success. Overlooked by Parliament, the House of Lords, the *ton*, and the merchant class, the men that would make up this clandestine organization stood to serve England under the command of a man who'd lost an arm and the sight in one eye for the cause.

"Lieutenant Frederick Langford and Mr. Tom Allen," Goodayle announced next.

Nelson's two aides stepped into the room.

"Danbury," Nelson said. "My condolences regarding the loss of your wife."

"Thank you, my lord." Simon swallowed thickly as he motioned for the vice-admiral to move farther into the room, dismissing his personal difficulties. They had no place here. He extended his hand. "We are ready."

"And they said it could not be done," Dundas interjected. "I shall be quite pleased to see my contemporaries in the War Office change their tune."

Goodayle reappeared with a tray of glasses filled with amber liquid that sloshed around as he made his way through the library from Nelson and his aides, to Simon and Dundas, and then to the men they'd assembled in the room, chief among them Percival Avery, the Marquess of Stanton; Lieutenant Henry Guffald; and Garrick, Viscount Seaton.

Vice-Admiral Nelson surveyed the room. He lifted his glass, as did the others. "To England!"

"To England!" the men repeated.

Nelson downed the liquor in one gulp. When Goodayle returned, Nelson placed the empty glass on the tray and reached for another. "I'm indebted to you . . . Goodayle, isn't it? It's not every day a man meets another who's actually chosen to step down the social ladder."

Goodayle beamed. "Every man should do his duty."

"You're a good egg, Wittingham," Nelson said, using Goodayle's real name as he patted him on the shoulder.

Simon nodded to Goodayle. "As you've said many times, my lord, 'To be sure, there is no doing anything—'"

"Without trying," Nelson finished. He studied Simon. "A man can do anything he sets his mind to do. And yet, there are many who do not see things the way you and I do, Danbury."

"I heartily agree," Simon said.

He would never forget his brother's words: *Presumptuous pup. Why can't Nelson's current squadrons of officers and sailors band together? Why must it be you?*

Because Nelson's seamen were needed elsewhere, he'd told his brother. Because British lives were at risk unless he, or someone else, kept Napoleon's armada from pirating or blockading trade and put an end to the plots against the monarchy.

"Stanton!" Simon hailed. "You are the first man I shall introduce."

Stanton left his position by the hearth, cocked his hip, and swaggered closer. "Egad," he said, jutting out his chin above his starched cravat. "I'm all aflutter to be in your presence, my good sir. What a fabulous honor it is to meet England's savior at last."

Nelson narrowed his good eye and studied Stanton. Today, he wore a powdered wig to flaunt his wealth—taxes on powder having increased—and he'd added a mole on his powdered cheek, next to his nose. A beribboned queue matched his flamboyant green-striped suit with its embroidered rose-colored waistcoat. His shoes had been spit-polished to a glistening sheen. He looked like a man who'd stepped out of an eighteenth-century painting.

Both ingenious and ridiculous.

It was a performance that left Simon no doubt that a warrior primed for battle lurked beneath the disguise. But Nelson didn't know that—yet.

Simon regarded Nelson. "May I present Percival Avery, the Marquess of Stanton."

"Your father is the Duke of Blendingham, is he not?" Nelson asked.

"You're quite astute, good fellow," Stanton said. "He's a member of the House of Lords."

"Will your participation pose a problem? You are the duke's only son, if I am not mistaken."

Percy tossed his quizzing glass upward, caught it with lightning-fast reflexes, stashed the fob in his waistcoat, and with a comical gyration of his hips, straightened his spine before accepting Nelson's extended hand. "My father has his way of serving the king; I have mine."

Nelson nodded, and another man stepped forward.

"Lieutenant Henry Guffald," Simon announced.

Blond, blue-eyed Guffald, his uniform pristinely ornamented, bowed and then sharply rose to attention. "It's my honor to be of service, my lord."

Nelson grinned at Langford. "Guffald reminds me of Lieutenant Parker." Parker had been one of Nelson's beloved aides-de-camp. "Damned unfortunate I lost the boy in Boulogne." He inspected Guffald. "An officer who wins the love of his men will work wonders where a leader of a different stamp will fail. Wisdom before honor, Lieutenant. Make me proud."

"Aye, my lord." Guffald nodded.

A tall, wide-shouldered man with long, loose-hanging hair and icy-blue eyes sauntered forward. He laid a jeweled hand on a silver sword scabbard at his wide leather belt and regarded Nelson's aides with distrust. "Garrick, Viscount Seaton, privateer, and the Earl of Pendrim's son," Simon said as he introduced the wayward, seafaring captain.

Seaton towered over Nelson by a head or more.

"Privateer, eh?" Nelson peered sideways at his aides, who suddenly appeared thunderstruck.

"Aye, sir. The best there is," he said proudly.

"Ah," Nelson said, stretching out his hand. Seaton took it and gave it a solid shake. "It will be good to have a man with your . . . experience on our side. War is beyond England's shores, not within it."

Seaton grinned. "I'm eager for a fight."

Simon introduced the remaining men he'd gathered: Captain Collins, Lieutenants Winters and Edwards, Clemmons, Stanley, Moore, Randall, Forsyth, Douglas, Whitbread, Russell, Milford, Holt, Walden, Chapman, and Hamlet. Vice-Admiral Nelson shook each man's hand. After a moment of contemplative silence, he asked, "Where is my Lady Nelson's twin?"

Simon furrowed his brows. "Who?"

"The courageous widow," he said, smiling. "You know, the one who warned us in the Theatre Royal."

"I am here," Gillian said, entering the library on cue, her black hair parted down the middle. She'd obviously taken great care to downplay her appearance, likely in an attempt to avoid drawing attention to herself in order to fit in—if that was possible in a room full of males. But the black gown only seemed to enhance her oval face and the intensity of her intelligent brown eyes. She'd failed miserably in Simon's mind. She would always be his light beckoning him from afar, no matter how long it took to properly grieve for his dear wife.

"Lord Nelson." Gillian walked up to the vice-admiral, bowed her head, and curtsied. "I pray my performance didn't disturb Lady Hamilton overmuch."

"On the contrary." Nelson puffed out his chest and rose on the balls of his feet as if to feign a greater height. She'd always been taller than the other ladies onstage. "Lady Nelson is a patient and forgiving sort, except when it comes to me," he said. "She prefers the country and I... well, I am energized by the masses."

Somehow Gillian doubted that any woman would appreciate being made a spectacle of while her husband cavorted with his paramour. She suspected it was the acclaim that the vice-admiral coveted, not the respect Simon had so willingly given Lady Danbury. "And Lady Hamilton?"

He smiled. "She is my saint."

Saint?

Gillian stiffened. Why did the use of that particular word cause her unease?

Of course! The man in the alley had used it! Could the word *saint* have something to do with the other man in the alley, a code name perhaps? He had asked for help. She'd have to investigate further.

"I am sure she is," Gillian agreed, smiling to cover the fact that her thoughts had wandered.

Nelson didn't look convinced. She prayed no one else had picked up on her reaction. It wouldn't do to fail muster before she'd even begun to earn her place among them.

"I do regret the hysterics, Admiral," she continued, "but I was—"

"In a thrall?" Nelson quirked his brow. He bowed. "Think on it no more. I daresay my dear wife, loyal soul that she is, would have done the same for me. Lady Nelson may be disagreeable and pious, but she is determined." His lips thinned, and he leaned forward conspiratorially, as if he hated what he was about to say. "*She* can do no wrong in the public's eyes."

Nelson was right. His wife comported herself with dignity, just as Simon's wife had. She was highly respected by the *ton*, though she wanted no part of the society Nelson craved. But what would Lady Fanny Nisbet Nelson think of Gillian sullying the woman's good name by causing a scene, even for such a worthy cause as saving her husband's life? Only time would tell.

Gillian had done many things to aid Lucien. Some she prayed she could forget, like being forced to kill. Others she hoped no one would ever discover. She'd played multiple roles, disguising herself as actresses, servants, tavern wenches, and widows long before pretending to be Vice-Admiral Nelson's wife. Though it had only been several days since she'd found Lucien in the woods, *that* woman, the one who'd held her dying husband in her arms, the one who'd fled her home and the gendarmes, didn't seem to exist. Could she continue being a covert agent for the Crown?

Yes. A thousand times, yes.

Truth be told, she craved the adventure, the danger. Perhaps that was what had drawn her to the stage in the first place. No two performances were ever alike. Something always seemed to change for better or worse, one never knew which. And like the stage actors who'd come before her, she thrived on it. She wouldn't abandon Simon. When she made a vow, she kept it. She'd stay, just as she'd promised Lady Danbury, even if it meant loving Simon from afar.

Love? Had the vines guarding her heart begun to bloom again?

The shock of her emotions hit her full force. Simon stood close by. His scent awakened her, mustering dormant desires she'd thought buried and gone forever. His consideration for her well-being, his gentle regard, and the promise of protection he'd made her broke down her defenses. She craved to be held by him, to be safe, warm, and assured that there was a reason to hope they could one day be together.

"Is that the sword that almost ended your life at Calvi in June of ninety-four, Danbury?" Dundas startled her out of her musings and pointed to the naval sword hanging in a case over the mantel. She glanced at Simon.

"Yes," Simon answered, a tic working in his jaw. He was anxious, she noticed, entirely too nervous for his own good. "Nearly lost my leg over it."

Gillian swallowed thickly, pushing the horrific image from her mind, and joined him at the sideboard. She beat him to the crystal decanter and took off the lid, the glass clinking. "More brandy, my lord?"

"What are you doing?" he asked, sneaking a look over his shoulder at the men in the room.

"Pouring you a drink." The brandy sloshed into his glass. "I . . . wanted to be the first to tell you that I accept the position you have offered me."

"You will join Nelson's Tea?" He swirled his brandy, taking his time and making a show of inhaling the liquor. "Our association will be unorthodox, to say the least."

"Perhaps." She set the decanter back on the bar. "Though, when has our relationship been anything but?"

His expression grew serious. "May I announce your decision?"

"Yes." Her heart leaped. "You may."

He nodded, lowering the tumbler to the bar. His fingers brushed her hand, sending prickling sparks of excitement through her.

"What do you think, Danbury?" Nelson asked, snapping her out of the moment. "Seaton believes Napoleon's blockades have been put in place to defy British trade and isolate us, as well as conceal the fact that he is smuggling gold out of England to fund his war." Nelson put his hands behind his back. "Seaton's contacts in Spain could actively investigate leads in San Sebastian to prove that suspicion. The city is only twelve miles from the French border, as you are well aware."

"I am, and I agree. Seaton would be the perfect agent for such an investigation." Simon's fingers brushed Gillian's again as he left her side. "Intuition has been your helpmate, Admiral. You have said many a time that 'following your own head, trusting your judgment is better than following the opinions of others.'"

"Though many in the Admiralty have questioned the admiral's procedures, I have never discounted his judgment," Dundas said, launching to his feet. "It is and always has been sound. That is why I am here. But how, in good conscience, will we fund such a venture? I cannot solicit money from naval reserves without fear of being taken to task."

"No one is asking you to endanger yourself, Dundas. Finance," Simon replied without inflection, "has already been arranged."

"By whom?" Gillian asked, feeling as if her head was on a swivel.

Nelson smiled. "Many of you have heard of Admiral Cochrane, the Master of Deception. Or as the Frenchies call him, *le Loup des Mers*."

"The Sea Wolf," Gillian exclaimed, earning Nelson's emphatic stare.

"Aye," Nelson said. "My good friend has outwitted the enemy time and again with his deceptions. We shall mimic Cochrane's strategy by sending out false information. The king has—"

"King George?" Dundas gasped. "Pardon me for saying so, but many in Parliament think His Majesty is not stable."

"My lord—" Gillian stepped toward the center of the room "—we must all take care in how we discuss matters of political import, especially when it concerns the king."

"I meant no disrespect." Dundas folded his hands together and inhaled deeply. "My chief concern is that the king does not suffer unnecessary prejudice if funding for Nelson's Tea becomes widely known. His authority must never come into question, especially now that the current prime minister, Henry Addington, is focused on foreign policy."

Nelson was in his element, and his appeal was not lost on Gillian. "The king does not fully support Addington." He began to move about the room, measuring up each man, his presence a stabilizing force that was hard to resist. "Addington is doubling the efficiency of tax reform. Napoleon and the pope have reached an accord, reconciling revolutionaries within the Catholic Church. France is building a fleet, which can only mean, after losing most of its capable officers to the guillotine or desertion, he plans to destroy the Royal Navy." He paused, allowing them all to absorb the information. "You can be sure that the French Consulate is doing everything within its power to cut England off from its allies, and they have every intention of conquering us. And as long as I have breath in my body, I will not sit back and watch it happen."

"I am responsible for His Majesty's ships and the resolute men who follow me to their graves," the vice-admiral said. "I am held accountable for the broken families war leaves behind. No, my good fellows, we must take the bull by the horns. We must prove, by actively protecting our shores, that our behavior is not dictated by fear, that we have no apprehension of the fate that lies ahead. It is our sovereign duty to gather facts, to keep secret our private signals, and to discover when the enemy will strike. You—" he pointed to each man and then leveled his finger at Gillian "—have been chosen. I do not seek another laurel for my post; I seek to achieve victory for my God and king."

Stanton stood, waved his quizzing glass, and shouted, "Hear! Hear!"

Gillian's heart pounded furiously as the rest of the men replied, "To death and glory!"

"I would have a toast," Nelson said loudly to end the reverie. "Where is Wittingham ... I mean Goodayle." He glanced at Gillian. "You must keep me on task, Baroness."

She nodded, her heart full. She was participating in something bigger than she'd ever imagined. Surrounded by tomes of wisdom, the room vibrated with energy barely leashed, and she knew she'd never forget this night.

Goodayle entered the room with another tray of drinks.

Nelson intercepted the man. "After everyone has a glass, put the tray down, Goodayle. I would have you join us."

Goodayle did as he was told, and within a matter of minutes, everyone was waiting expectantly for the vice-admiral to speak.

"Do you agree to uphold the monarchy and protect England, be it as a peer, officer, smuggler, publisher, shipmaster, miller, paymaster, artist, vicar, or seductress?" he asked, winking at Gillian.

She took no offense. "Aye," she said, adding her voice to the rest.

Nelson paused, then raised his glass. "To England."

"To England," they replied.

The vice-admiral studied them above the rim of his glass as they all took a drink. "The enemy will not have reason to boast of their security. For I trust, ere long, to assist them in person in a way that will completely annihilate the whole of them."

Gillian glanced around the room. The spies Simon had handpicked, the challenges they would face in the future, gave her pause. Would any of them survive the daunting task that lay ahead? There were no guarantees. Lucien was proof of that.

"England expects that every man, and woman," Nelson said, giving Gillian a nod, "will do his or her duty."

She'd given everything for her country. Was she prepared to lose Simon, too?

"Hear! Hear!" they shouted. "To death and glory!"

Gillian turned to Simon, her burden growing heavier. From stagehand, to actress, to baroness and spy, she never could have imagined the direction her life had taken or the dramatic turn her life would now take.

Eleven

"Is second childishness and mere oblivion,
Sans teeth, sans eyes, sans taste, sans everything . . ."
~William Shakespeare, As You Like It

FOG OBSCURED MANY of the tombstones in St. Luke's Cemetery as the mist crept over the wintry landscape from the river. The somber gloom pressed in on Simon as the pall was removed from Edwina's pine coffin, revealing the brass plate inscribed with her name and dates of birth and death, and he prepared to say a final goodbye before she was lowered into the consecrated ground. He wasn't accustomed to living in the present but rather by anticipating whatever tomorrow would bring in order to save lives. He had no other choice in this moment, however. The burden of not being able to give Edwina the life she'd deserved weighed heavy on his chest, achoring him to the cold, unforgiving ground. At least now, he could gift her with a royal end to years of torment and pain.

Mr. Crofton, the officiating vicar, finished reading from the Good Book. "Amen." He made the sign of the cross and nodded to Simon before moving aside.

Simon stood motionless, a white mist materializing before his mouth with each breath. A sennight had passed since Edwina's death, and November had brought a bracing chill carrying a promise of snow. In the interim, her body had been dressed and laid out in the town house beneath a woolen shroud surrounded by flowers. The scent of the flowers, he'd been told, would help relieve his niece Constance's and Lady Landon-Fitzhugh's sensibilities as they sat vigil over her body. Edwina's mother's stamina was low. Her sadness, and the risk the cold posed to her health, denied her the closure attending her daughter's funeral would bring.

He grimaced. It was deuced hard to be stoic in public, but enduring pain had been drilled into him from childhood. He'd been called on, at various times in his life—as he was today—to use that strength when the occasion warranted it. The current social methodology fancied that women couldn't control themselves at graveside services. Tradition often prevented the opposite sex from attending particular events, and it filled him with disgust. Women could do just about anything they put their minds to. Hadn't Gillian proved that to be the case?

Simon exhaled, producing another white cloud of frozen air. He stood among friends: Stanton, Goodayle, Archer, and his brother, Rock. Vice-Admiral Nelson had retired to Number Twenty-Three Piccadilly for several days and then planned to head to Merton, the new home he'd purchased to share with the Hamiltons. Simon didn't fully understand the nature of the Hamiltons' relationship with the vice-admiral, nor did he care. The navy had taught him to concentrate on his own matters instead of desiring to be privy to what went on in other people's beds. Lord knew he'd always had problems of his own to master.

Dundas, on the other hand, had returned to Whitehall while the other members of Nelson's Tea had returned to their places of origin to begin the first of many missions for King George III, Nelson, and Sir Arthur Wellesley.

Sir Landon-Fitzhugh raised a handkerchief to his mouth

and coughed loudly, clearing his lungs. He wore a black overcoat, a black beaver hat, and a black armband. Simon and the rest of the men present wore a similar style.

Well-wishers stepped forward and laid lilies on Edwina's coffin. They offered their condolences, shook Simon's hand, and then departed. He thanked each of the mourners who'd traveled to Chelsea on this cold, blustery day. Edwina's life may have been extinguished at thirty years of age, but she left a legacy of compassion and charity never to be forgotten and a brand on his heart.

Frost crunched beneath the retreating feet of the guests who retired to their conveyances. Ropes screeched against Edwina's coffin as the time to lower her into the holy ground finally came. The air was crisp. Prayers were murmured, each one splintering his icy facade. He'd prayed for Edwina often into the night, but not all prayers were answered the way one wanted them to be.

Rock laid a hand on Simon's shoulder, startling him out of his trance. "It's time," his brother said.

Simon nodded woodenly. He stepped forward and reached down for a handful of soil. He weighed the sediment in his hand, feeling the urge to take off his gloves and grasp the earth with his bare fingers. But he didn't. To do so ignited his emotions. He couldn't bear to imagine what life would have been like for them both had Edwina not been frail. Instead, he summoned strength from an unknown well, tossed the soil over his wife's coffin, and watched the brass plate disappear.

A breeze caressed his hair where it grazed the top of his cravat, reminding him of Edwina's touch. He closed his eyes and saw Edwina's face.

Live, Simon. Go to her. Her last request filled him with regret but also a sense of purpose. In time, he could let go. Until then, he would plant a lush carpet of flowers over her grave so that her final resting place would bring others the kind of beauty and blessing she'd been in her prime.

Stanton and Goodayle stood with Archer, who'd been devoted to Edwina. Archer motioned to Simon. "My lord?"

Simon brushed off his gloves and turned away from his wife's grave as the diggers committed to their arduous task. "I am ready."

They turned and walked away but not toward the vehicles where the black jobbers—the funeral procession masters—waited by three teams of Friesian horses. There was still another burial to attend today.

They moved to the plot where Gillian stood by another black-draped coffin, wind playing with her veil. Simon frowned. Burying men who'd followed his orders would surely be the part of his job he detested. How could he say goodbye to a man who'd sacrificed his life for his God, king, and country? For without the baron's help, they truly might not have learned of the plan to assassinate Vice-Admiral Nelson.

Drawn to Gillian, Simon knew that she'd breached tradition by coming to say her final goodbyes to her husband, and his feet moved of their own volition. He studied her as he approached. She was dressed in a black cloak and a black turban with a long veil fringed with bugles, looking as stiff as the limestone markers.

Mr. Crofton fell into step beside him. "Are you not pleased, my lord?"

Simon stopped and repositioned his cane, feeling suddenly ill at ease. He flexed his fingers around the silver dragon's head handle and looked down at the rotund reverend, wanting to throttle the man. Why, he couldn't be sure. Was a man supposed to be pleased that he was burying his wife or that a man had died trying to warn them all?

"What do you mean, vicar?" Simon asked, tempering his

mounting frustration.

"With the service," the man quickly explained, as if realizing his blunder. "That is to say . . . what I mean is, the number of people in attendance on a cold, foggy day such as this . . ."

"It is always cold and foggy in England."

The vicar raised his brows.

"Forgive me," Simon said. "This has been a strain on my constitution. If it weren't for the ridiculous custom of not allowing women to attend funerals, I daresay there would not have been any room around Lady Danbury's grave. She was loved and respected by many."

Mr. Crofton's face reddened. "Of course. She will find no better final resting place than St. Luke's." The man gulped when Simon simply stared at him. "As I'm aware you already know. Ah," he said, holding out his hand, "I see that our next funeral is ready to begin. If you will allow me to, I'll proceed with the reading."

Allow him? The baron was Gillian's husband, not his. Still, he nodded and said, "Of course."

The sound of dirt plunking atop Edwina's coffin followed Simon as he limped the seventy paces that would bring him to Gillian's side. Life was given and taken, born to sunrise and set to bittersweet memories. The distance between them loomed large, an infernal gap that he meant to narrow without causing any impropriety.

Gillian's veil covered her face allowing him little in the way of seeing her expression fully as he walked toward her, though the reason they were there and the way she clasped her gloved hands together spoke volumes. She stood silent and unyielding, a picture of grace and bereavement as she stared into the depths of what would be Chauncey's final resting place.

Stanton, Goodayle, and Archer turned to look at the road as Sir Landon-Fitzhugh's carriage retreated. Simon, too, watched the horses trot off, hooves clomping on the lane and the suspension complaining.

Rock put his hand on his brother's shoulder once more. "It was good of you to send for the baron's body, Dan," he said. "I realize I didn't offer my support when the duke arranged your marriage, but I know how deeply the baroness's marriage to another man affected you."

"I had the means to help her, that is all."

"Is it?" Rock peered into his eyes. "Most men would not honor the man who married the woman he once loved." He smiled sadly when Simon opened his mouth to deny his words. "Say no more. I understand better than most. True love does not fade with time or even death."

"There is more here than meets the eye." Simon grabbed Rock's hand and squeezed it tightly. His brother didn't know about the way he'd lived his life or exactly what he did for the Admiralty, but to protect him and Constance, Simon needed to keep it that way. "We are not most men."

"No." His brother winked. "We are not. And so I shall leave you in the vicar's care. Cooper and the rest of the staff have prepared Throckmorton for us. Do come for refreshments. It will do you good."

Simon nodded. "Thank you, Brother."

Rock made his way to his carriage, a black landau that had been shined so clean it reflected the tombstones and crypts nearby.

Ding. Ding. Ding.

Simon looked away from his brother's conveyance and lifted his gaze to the steeple as the death knell began. The church's melodic carillon was a haunting reminder of how fleeting life could be. That no one was immortal. Certainly not spies who willingly put themselves in danger.

"It is done," Simon whispered to Gillian as he came to a stop beside her.

His thoughts were jagged and painful as he waited for her to alert him that she'd heard him speak, though her closeness was a comfort and a relief. As much as he'd prepared for Edwina's death, there was emptiness inside him that only faith in God, time, and the love he'd once shared with Gillian could fill. He stood as close to her as decorum allowed as they listened to the bells chime and then slowly fade.

When at last a solemnity settled back over the graveyard, Gillian looked at Simon for the first time since he'd left Edwina's graveside. "The bells . . . are a nice touch, my lord. Please offer my thanks to the ringers."

"I will," he promised.

She sighed. "I've been standing here for some time, just listening to the wind."

"Are you not cold?"

"No. This is a peaceful place. Your wife and my husband will like it here, and I must thank you for it."

"There is nothing to thank me for."

"You sent for the baron's body," she insisted.

It was true, but he'd done so without expecting thanks. "It was disagreeable that he be buried without any fanfare. I did what any man would do."

"You forget I've seen men at their worst," she said.

Did she refer to him, as well? Would she ever forgive him for marrying another?

"Perhaps," he said softly.

"I speak honestly. You see things other men do not. The baron and I began our lives here. How just and fitting that this is the place our time together comes to an end."

Beginnings always have endings.

Their gazes met, and guilt sheared away from Simon's shoulders. "Death is not the end, Gillian. Your husband will live on . . . in you, in me—"

"In all of us," Stanton finished as he stepped closer. "Pardon me for eavesdropping, but I'd hoped to draw your attention elsewhere."

Gillian cut her gaze to the marquess. Simon thought he saw a haunting smile beneath her veil. He turned to spy what Gillian had seen to lift her spirits so.

He didn't need long to find out. There, all around them, men marched in a procession out of the trees from the direction of the river and through the headstones, entering the graveyard from every direction, dressed in black greatcoats with matching armbands—the members of Nelson's Tea.

"What is this?" he asked, dumbfounded. "I was told the men had all gone home."

Stanton somehow managed to look the part of effeminate fop as he cocked out his hip, even dressed in dull black garments. "We swore an oath, did we not, to stand together come what may?"

Simon nodded. "We did."

"Did you think we would dishonor one of our fallen by allowing him to be put to rest without a proper farewell?"

Gillian held her head high as Viscount Seaton, naval officers Guffald, Winters, Edwards, and Collins, Whitbread, Russell, Milford, Holt, Walden, Chapman, and Hamlet, and the four other men who'd joined the clandestine group came to her, bowed, and took their places around Chauncey's grave.

Simon and Gillian both turned as a team of Friesian horses pulling a black carriage with gold embellishment arrived. The footman stepped down, lowered the steps, and opened the door. Inside the carriage, Simon saw a man put on his bicorn. Then lowering his head to fit through the framework, Vice-Admiral Nelson exited the vehicle. He stood by and waited for another man to follow. When his companion, Henry Dundas, joined him, the two men marched toward the graveside.

They stopped before Chauncey's coffin and gave a salute, then offered Gillian their condolences before taking their places beside Simon.

"Your fortitude is remarkable, Baroness." Nelson's rich baritone was controlled. "If only every woman in our nation could summon such strength."

"It is of necessity," she said. "I am greatly honored you came, my lord. Thank you. Thank you all."

"It is I who am honored, my lady," Nelson said, stepping back as the funeral assistants removed the pall from Chauncey's coffin.

Simon was astonished at the awe brimming inside him. He'd never been prouder than he was at this moment. The men he and the vice-admiral had assembled had come to show their respect for a man who'd blazed a trail for them to follow. If this was any indication of how well they would all work together, he could—and would—be content.

Mr. Crofton moved to the head of the grave. "Now that we are all here, shall we begin?" He cleared his throat and eased his spectacles down his nose. "Out of the deep have I called unto thee . . ." The vicar's prayer continued for several minutes and ended with, "And in Him there is plenteous redemption."

Simon looked to Gillian as he stood beside her in a show of unity. Theirs was a union he hoped to one day rekindle, and intended to honor until the day he died. They were professionals in a perilous field that often courted folly. The risk that neither of them would survive was great. But somehow fate had brought them back together, and by god, he would not allow anyone to tear them asunder.

When the moment came to ease the baron's coffin into the ground, Gillian's lower lip quivered slightly. Daring to offer her what comfort he could, he reached for her hand. He was stepping out of bounds of propriety, but he wanted her to know that she wasn't alone. That she'd never be alone.

She jerked her hand away, clasping her fingers in front of her again.

The vicar gave Simon a nod. It was time to say goodbye.

He guided her forward with one motion, his hand on her elbow. She grabbed a handful of soil in her kid glove and turned, hesitating only briefly as she dropped the earth on the baron's coffin.

"We should go," he told her when the service was finished. "The sky is darkening and the air has grown colder." He could feel the chill in his bones and as exhausted as he knew she was, he didn't want her to catch the ague.

"Wait," she said, turning to look at the men standing a respectful distance from her. "Thank you for honoring my husband. I shall never forget it."

The men tipped their hats, offering more condolences, and then, just as silently and suddenly as they had appeared, they returned the way they had come.

Simon placed Gillian's hand in the crook of his arm and watched the others go as the church bells rang once more.

Gillian tilted her head to look at him. "How much did you pay the bell ringers?"

He shrugged and glanced at the steeple where the bells were housed. "A significant donation. But in this instance, money is no consequence."

"But the expense," she exclaimed. "Surely—"

"Worth every pound note," he interrupted. With agonizing slowness, he tore his gaze from the bell tower and looked down at Gillian while he escorted her to the carriage. "My brother and his daughter have prepared refreshments for us." The black beasts pawed the ground in anticipation of their arrival. "Shall we away?" he asked, helping her up the steps.

She climbed inside and sat back on the squabs. "Is that

wise?"

He joined her. "Do you recall what the admiral said before our meeting in the library disbanded? 'We mustn't allow fear to dictate how we live our lives. And we must not live with the apprehension of what this day has in store for us.'"

She raised her veil. "You quote Nelson's code now?"

"One—nothing is predictable." He got up and moved beside her as the carriage began to move. "We have lived different lives, matured and loved with no regrets."

"Yes," she slowly agreed. "Go on."

"Two—flexibility saves lives." He brought her gloved fingers to his lips. "In spite of our past, imagine the good we can achieve as a united front."

She drew back her hand. "I wasn't aware that we were the only members of Nelson's Tea," she said.

"Three"—he added swiftly—"be on hand . . . to assist friends."

"Simon," she whispered, determination knitting her brows. "Be advised, I am prepared to—"

"Four"—he cut in—"deliberate your options."

"You are incorrigible," she protested, looking away. After a moment's hesitation, she glanced back at him. "What options?"

"The future holds many possibilities for both of us." He cupped her face. "Five—execute every decision with astonishing heroism." He stroked her cheek with his thumb. "From this moment forward, everything we say and do will be suspect."

"Our bereavement—"

"Will be met," he finished for her. "As it should be." He wouldn't scandalize her or dishonor the ones they loved. "But these are dangerous times. We have no idea when a mission will be our last. I do not want to squander what time we do have. And if I am to be honest with you—and I vow I always will be—I must confess a long-held secret."

"What secret?" she asked.

"You stole my heart years ago, and I have never wanted it back."

"Oh, Simon." Her eyes darkened with pain. "If only things had been different for us."

He shook his head. "We cannot go back. I only ask that I may be given a second chance to love you in the future."

She smiled, color returning to her features. "It won't be easy. There are people who will talk." Not unless they gave them reason to, that was. She placed her hands in his. "I never wanted any of this . . ."

"Don't." He put his finger on her lips. "Let me finish. There is no way around it. We will—we must—mourn our spouses for as long as it takes. I would never expect anything less." He inhaled her scent, drowning in the bittersweet agony of finding his first love at the cost of losing another. "When Edwina lay dying, she asked me to go to you, to love you . . . to live."

"What did you tell her?" she asked.

"That I would. You understand what that means, don't you?"

The corners of her mouth turned upward. "I believe so."

"I do not take my vows lightly. She thought of nothing else but my happiness in the end, and I will spend my life upholding the promise I made to her." He cupped the sides of her face and looked deeply into her eyes. "I will never be persuaded to leave you again."

"Oh, Simon." Tears glistened in her eyes. She raised his hands to her lips and kissed him. "Your wife urged me to forgive you. She gave me her blessing, too."

"Then it is settled," he said, sitting back on the squabs. "We've been given our heading. Our sails are set."

"It would appear so." She smiled again. "If this accounts

for anything, please know that I will always be indebted to you for introducing me to Lucien, Simon. I am who I am today because of him."

"And how glad I am of it," he said sincerely. Without the covert training Lucien had provided Gillian, Simon might never have seen her alive again. "Lucien has always had my utmost respect."

"You are kind."

"No, I'm a rogue through and through, and never forget it."

"Several rogues would be needed to defeat Fouché's men. It will not be easy to accomplish all that the admiral requires." She hinted at their travails ahead. "Among our successes, there are bound to be losses. Difficult days await us both."

"I can endure it as long as I do not lose you again," he admitted, pulling her close. He brushed her veil out of his face. "I could not survive it."

"Then for reasons I will not share at this time, I will endeavor to live."

Emotions dueled inside Simon as he tightened his arms about Gillian. "And I will hold you to that promise."

Author's note

THE IDEA FOR the Nelson's Tea Series came to me while researching Vice-Admiral Lord Horatio Nelson and the political upset of the Napoleonic Wars (1795-1815). Nelson's courage in the face of adversity was inspiring. He was a glory seeker, a vain man struggling to rise in the ranks at a time when promotions were earned at a grueling pace. Few rivaled his bravery, and nothing—including losing sight in his right eye at Calvi or his right arm at Santa Cruz de Tenerife—could stop him from doing his duty.

He was also adored by the masses, craved constant attention, and loved in earnest. And there was one thing Nelson never went without: his tea. He drank tea at the same time every day, even while aboard a ship or in battle. That's when the idea hit me. What if when Nelson asked for his tea, he meant a mercenary group operating outside of the Admiralty's reach? What if the group consisted of men who defied convention, men unafraid to risk their lives for king and country? And what if they were men from every walk of life, or the kind of men who lived and roved outside the law? What if they were *pirates*?

And that was it. I just *had* to write that story. Before I start writing any of my historical romance novels, though, I always research, and while doing so, I always find fabulous nuggets of information. One such instance is the production of Holcroft's *Deaf and Dumb*, originally produced by Holcroft, T. & Bouilly, J. N. (1801). *Deaf and Dumb,* or *The Orphan Protected* is an historical drama in five acts, which was first performed by Their Majesties Servants of the Theatre Royal in Drury Lane on February 24, 1801. Vice-Admiral Lord Horatio Nelson returned to London on October 22, 1801 due to ill-health, took up residence with Lord William and Emma Hamilton at Twenty-Three Piccadilly, and spoke out in support of Prime Minister Addington in the House of Lords particularly between October 29 and November 12, 1801. Two plays are listed as having been produced at Drury Lane in 1801: Holcroft's *Deaf and Dumb* (February 1801) and Lewis's *Adelmourn the Outlaw* (May 1801). It is here that I took literary license and moved the production of Holcroft's play to November 5, 1801. This was a time of peace, a time when Nelson wished all Frenchmen to the devil, and a perfect time for Napoleon to strike while the enemy was asleep.

Resources used in my research for this book include the following:

The Cambridge Companion to British Theatre, 1730-1830

Plays About the Theatre in England, 1737-1800

Lewis's *Adelmourn the Outlaw*, May 4, 1801, Drury Lane

The Illegitimate Theatre in London, 1770-1840

The History of Productions of *Venice Preserv'd* Website

The Theatre Royal, Drury Lane Website

Acknowledgments

MY BOOKS WOULDN'T have the swashbuckling action, humor, and adventure I strive to include without the help of my brainstorming partner, author M.V. Freeman. Our plotting sessions and satisfying afternoon teas are the joy of my life. Thank you, dear friend!

Special thanks to the other authors who helped plot this series, Crystal R. Lee and Jean Hovey. I'd also like to thank Nicole Laverdure, Monique Daoust, and Liette Bougie for helping me with the French translations in this series. *Merci!!!* And thanks go out to Ingrid Seymour for the Spanish translations. *Gracias!*

Behind every good book is a FABulous team. Thank you from the bottom of my heart to Jennifer Lawler, Adams Media, Kim Bowman, and EsKape Press who believed in me when no one else would. And thank you to my dream team at Double Vision Editorial, my editors Danielle Poiesz, Lorrie Noggle, and Kyle Avery. You've taken my stories to the next level! Huzzah!

Raising a well-deserved signal flag to my Rogues, Rebels & Rakes Street Team and all my fans on social media! Thank you for sharing this extraordinary voyage with me!

Lastly, I owe everything I am and achieve to God and my family, whose love and support enable me to spend countless hours at my computer doing this thing that I love so much. To my family and to you, dear reader, thank you for sharing my passion for swashbuckling heroes of yesteryear!

–Katherine

About the Author

HISTORICAL ROMANCE AUTHOR **Katherine Bone** has been passionate about history since she had the opportunity to travel to various Army bases, castles, battlegrounds, and cathedrals as an Army brat turned officer's wife. Who knew an Army wife's passion for romance novels would lead to pirates? Certainly not her rogue, whose Alma Mater's adage is "Go Army. Beat Navy!" Now enjoying the best of both worlds, Katherine lives with her hero in the south, where she writes about rogues, rebels, and rakes—aka pirates, lords, captains, duty, honor, and country—and the happily-ever-afters that every alpha male and damsel deserve.

Katherine's FAN Mail:
katherine@katherinebone.com

Katherine on the web:
www.katherinebone.com

Katherine's Official Facebook FAN Page:
facebook.com/Katherine-Bones-Official-Fan-Page-134578253291785

Katherine's BookBub Page:
bookbub.com/authors/katherine-bone

Katherine on Twitter:
twitter.com/katherinelbone

Thank you for reading *My Lord Rogue*!

Dear Reader,

I HOPE YOU enjoyed Simon and Gillian's mission to save Vice-Admiral Nelson's life, and their heart wrenching love story. I understand the ending of book isn't the traditional HEA you might have been expecting. Don't worry though! This introduction to my Nelson's Tea Series sets the ground work for Simon and Gillian to have their HEA in ***My Lady Rogue***, and it's a beautiful one, I promise you that! Until then, reviews are a great way for readers like yourself to find books, and I'd be ever so grateful if you took the time to share your experience with others.

Interested in knowing when my next book will be available? Sign up for Katherine's Rogues, Rebels & Rakes E-Newsletter. www.katherinebone.com/contact

Keep reading for a sneak peek at the next book in the Nelson's Tea Series, ***Duke by Day, Rogue by Night***, featuring Percival Avery, the Duke of Blendingham, and Simon's niece, Lady Constance Danbury.

Percy's quest to avenge his family puts him at odds with his commander's niece, a woman who faces her greatest fear and is suddenly thrust into danger.

One

The English Channel, 1804

"HANDS TO QUARTERS," the bosun shouted.

More orders filtered down from the quarterdeck through the companionway to the deck below. The merchantman they'd been searching for was finally within range. Grappling hooks were plied from the mizzenmast and boarding pikes, pistols, and swords were removed from their hidey-holes.

Percival Avery, the Duke of Blendingham, strode through the passageway of the *Striker's* gun deck, dodging crewmen scurrying to their stations. Every man prepared to wreak havoc on the unsuspecting ship and the innocents harbored within the *Octavia's* pristine hull.

God help the poor wretches . . .

Dodging a member of the gun crew, Percy growled low in his throat as he swallowed back his disgust. If he showed his true colors now, everything he and the men loyal to him had hoped to achieve by putting an end to Captain Barnabas Frink's devious smuggling schemes would be lost. He longed to warn Frink's target of its impending doom, but under the circumstances, it was necessary for him to maintain his disguise. War loomed on the horizon, and far more lives weighed in the balance than would perish in this fight. So to nullify Frink's reign of terror and discover who was funding his forays into smuggling, Percy had to become the thing most seafaring men despised most—a pirate.

Hastening his footsteps, Percy approached Frink's cabin. He'd been summoned to report on the *Striker's* progress, as before. This time, however, there was more at stake. Every knot navigated toward the Bay of Biscay and their quarry brought them closer to a cargo ship bearing an English flag. The air frizzled with tension. Betrayal and disloyalty gutted him afresh. The *Octavia* was a prize the captain had been ordered to capture, and Frink had been promised a glorious reward for its return. Who commanded Frink, Percy wasn't privy to know. As the *Striker's* quartermaster, a man who'd earned Frink's highest regard, Percy didn't necessarily have the captain's ear, even though the captain relied on him. A more villainous man he'd never met. Every pore of the man's pock-ridden face oozed a hatred that poisoned all those under his command, including Percy, making him fear for his own mortal soul.

He knocked twice on the cabin bulkhead.

"Enter," the captain said sharply.

Percy lifted the latch and stepped inside, shutting out the calamitous activity along the gun deck as cannons were positioned on their breeching trucks and rolled out to volley deadly broadsides. Men scurried across the deck carrying powder cartridges to their houses. Aware of the captain's disdain for interruption, Percy closed the cabin door swiftly behind him. Time being of the essence, he was fueled by a need to discover for whom Frink plundered and why. No doubt a schemer was involved, a man bent on enriching his coffers; however, it could not be done without bloodying his hands. Luckily, Frink gladly fulfilled the task.

The captain was motivated by more than greed and lust. He had no decency whatsoever, no moral compass. He'd do anyone's bidding for the right price, including murder—or perhaps especially murder. An investigation into Frink's affairs had proven he was politically linked to someone in the House of Lords or Parliament, as well as to seditious Irish rebels and their treasonous acts. But who was this Englishman who controlled the captain like a marionette? Someone did. Percy had no proof to back his suspicions yet, but Frink certainly wasn't acting alone.

Eerie quiet met his ears. He confronted the captain, completely unfazed by the man's unpredictable demeanor. Unlike most men on board the *Striker*, Percy had the means of protecting himself, if it came to that, so he didn't fear the man as most did. In fact, Percy was choosing not to kill Frink, at least not until the time was right.

Frink didn't appear disturbed by his presence. He made no effort to acknowledge Percy. He was seated calmly at his desk, ignoring the haphazard footfalls above their heads. And why wouldn't he? Killing and maiming innocents was Frink's forte, with pilfering and plundering ships a normal occurrence.

The most detestable man to set sail since Francois L'Ollonais—who whipped, beat, and burned men alive—rose from his chair and shrugged his meaty form into his maroon brocade coat, before eyeing Percy irritably. "Well, don't stand there like a spindle-shanked whiffler. What's the hubbub about? Report yer findin's. Have we caught our prey? Are the men ready?"

"Aye," Percy said.

He strode forward, curbing his inclination to grab one of the swords from the bulkhead nearby and run Frink through. That satisfying act would save humanity much unnecessary grief and heaven the mournful wails of souls not long for this world. Percy fisted his hands, resisting the urge to choke the life out of the bastard. Instead, he came to a halt before Frink's overly large, masterfully crafted mahogany desk. Its four legs were adorned with garish carvings, and he studied them while he waited for the captain to speak. His conscience argued against allowing the attack to continue, but Nelson's Tea had reasons for backing the madman's scheme.

Damn my soul to hell.

"Out with it!" Frink shouted. "It's obvious ye have more to say. I can see it in yer eyes. How many guns does she have?"

"'Tis a twenty-four-gun merchantman," he said, allowing that information to sink in. "The *Octavia*, just as ye predicted. By all accounts, she's undermanned and shouldn't be difficult to board."

"The *Octavia*," Frink repeated thoughtfully, fingering his beard. His eyes flickered wickedly as he stared back at Percy. "Ye're certain?"

"Sure as death." Percy swallowed the bile rising in his throat. His chest tightened painfully, and he felt the weight of his duplicity as keenly as the beat of his own heart. He knew more than he wanted to know about death, and he warranted he'd witness plenty of it this very day.

He wasn't unfamiliar with piracy and all that the dangerous lifestyle entailed, and this wasn't his first foray into dangerous waters. He was one of the founding members of Nelson's Tea, a clandestine group organized by Lord Simon Danbury and Vice-Admiral Horatio Nelson to defend England's shores in 1801. His presence aboard the *Striker* coincided with an intricate plot to deceive and destroy anyone in league with their enemy, Napoleon. Percy had been sent to unmask Frink's secret employer, who they suspected associated with Napoleon in his efforts to cripple the British government. If the head of a snake wasn't cut off, it did little good to grab its tail.

Several of the captain's voyages had been linked to France, a treasonous association by all accounts. Nelson's Tea labored to curtail invasions of England, especially when the

French emperor was in such dire need of gold to fund his resurgence of war.

Frink thumbed through the pamphlets and maps on his desk. His lips twisted cruelly, making Percy regret inventing his alias, the pirate Thomas Sexton. "The moment has come. It'll be there. Mark my words."

"What will, sir?" he pressed, hoping to uncover some of the information he needed. "I thought the plan was to pillage the *Octavia* and sell her wares."

Frink cackled and jabbed his finger in the air. "Never ye mind, wharf rat!" He combed his fingers through his beard. "Leave the strategy to me." He locked his gaze with Percy's. "But harken this. I'll trust this prize with no other but ye."

Percy's brow furrowed, eyes crinkling in confusion. "Me?"

Someone shouted a warning above, just before a cannon shot whirred past the ship. The obvious miss hit the water off the starboard tack, causing the *Striker* to list side to side. Frink's face reddened. He let out a growl. "I've a score to settle with that cap'n for firin' on my ship." He cut his gaze to Percy. "When the attack begins, board her. Take yer men below and bring up what ye find to me. I'll do the rest."

"What if we're sailin' into a trap?" After all, he and his men were trying to trap Frink themselves.

The captain burst out laughing. "Ye've a quick mind. 'Tis one of the things I admire about ye." He left the haven of his cabin. "Leverage, Sexton. Never agree to a partnership or go into battle without it. Leverage gives a man the upper hand, especially when he's in a bind. And so it is with me. My employer has high aspirations, and I shall strip from him that which he desires most. That'll burn and blast his bones."

"Whose bones?" he asked, growing more confused than ever as an explosive burst of gunfire jolted the *Striker*. The situation was getting out of hand. He'd infiltrated Frink's crew with twenty men associated with Nelson's Tea under his command. Together, they'd clandestinely searched the ship for clues, questioned the crew, and listened to tall tales about the captain's nefarious activities, all the while hoping to put a stop to them.

"'Tis a woman we're after," Frink said, affirming the captain was about to cross the line. "One of my scouts in Wapping learned of her presence aboard the *Octavia* and notified me. Her name was confirmed in the manifest."

"She was the reason for our quick departure? This is all about a woman?"

Burn and skin me alive. Who the hell was she?

"Aye, she's . . ." The captain faltered. He glanced up at Percy, forcing him to mask his emotions before Frink could decipher them. Frink shook his head, a strange expression distorting his face. "Nay." He waved his hands outward. "Think on it no more. The less ye know the better. I've been promised a good purse. '*Dead or alive,*' he said. I'll collect either way." His eyes gleamed wickedly. "But I'd prefer the woman to be alive when she's captured." He allowed Percy time for his words to sink in. "That is where ye come in. Understood?"

Completely.

"Ye don't have any intention on deliverin' her alive, do ye?" Percy asked.

Frink cocked his brow, shrugged his broad shoulders, and bent to another task, easily dismissing the conversation.

History proved the captain would show little mercy to those aboard the *Octavia*, especially a woman. So why would someone want Frink to kidnap her? He intended to find out. If Frink's previous history was any indication, he would rake the *Octavia*, destroy her masts, and immobilize her, giving Percy time to acquire his prisoner. Then, Frink would use her cruelly, an act that would only prolong her agony. He couldn't allow it. He had to get to her first, discover what made her so valuable to Frink's source, and find a way to save her life.

He had not been able to save his sister, Celeste, or their father when they'd been ambushed in their carriage. God's hounds! Three months ago, his father's body had been found in the wreckage, his sister's nearby. Both had suffered cruelly at the hands of highwaymen, but Celeste more so. Her wounds suggested she'd fought her attackers, but she had clearly failed, suffering unconscionable pain instead. It was bad enough that Percy had not been able to locate the men responsible for their deaths, despite tirelessly searching for clues since the day he had learned what happened. He could not let that type of abuse happen to another woman, whether he knew her or not. It no longer mattered that he desperately needed Frink and the man, or men, who sanctioned his activities.

Oh, these were brutal times. In addition to gathering intelligence on Frink's correspondence, Percy had memorized maps and studied routes Frink had used between France and Dover, Plymouth and Saint-Malo. Whoever financed his money-making schemes waged war against England by funding Frink's gold-smuggling endeavors. While Percy and the other members of Nelson's Tea were trying to bring Frink and his benefactor to their knees, Napoleon would not stop until Britain was isolated from the rest of the world and destroyed from within.

Questions multiplied in his mind. Why would a lofty Englishman join forces with Captain Frink and the enemy in the first place? What did anyone have to gain with that association, other than financial stability, when there was infinitely more to lose? Hadn't enough men died already? Perhaps that didn't matter. Great men were not born; they were carried on the backs of innocents they crushed beneath them.

Sacrifices made to gather evidence thus far had already been great. Many good men had been lost, though none had affected him as deeply as the death of the man who'd taught Percy everything he knew about espionage, Lucien, Baron Chauncey. Percy may have been trained to accept loss of life, but the reality of a life spent in espionage was getting harder to bear, the weight heavier each and every day.

By birth, Percy was the only son of Rathbone Avery, Fourth Duke of Blendingham. As a duke's son, born into a life of privilege and ease, his secret identity allowed him freedoms his title did not. Thomas Sexton had materialized out of a need to investigate the East End, enabling him to shed his cloak of civility and operate covertly on overcrowded streets and in ill-favored slums, where he gleaned intelligence that benefited the clandestine group. Together, his two personas breeched the social divide, allowing him to mingle in Society and among docks and workhouses at will.

Flexibility saves lives. Nelson's Tea's second principle of conduct reminded him to always be prepared to alter his course at any given time. That time had come.

GENTLY BRED WOMEN did not disobey their fathers. But Lady Constance Danbury embraced rebellion with open arms the day she boarded a merchantman bound for Spain. A series of failed investments were threatening the reputation of her father, the Duke of Throckmorton, and his solution to rectify the situation required her to wed a much older, quite despicable man who'd tricked her, tried to kiss her, and then threatened to ruin Papa when she had refused his advances. But at nineteen, Constance refused to sacrifice herself and had been forced to come up with an alternative plan.

She could only think of one fix, however: to acquire her deceased mother's trust, which totaled thirty thousand pounds. Yet letters to her aunt, Lady Lydia Claremont Vasquez, had gone unanswered, and the woman was in charge of the funds until Constance's twenty-first birthday. Aunt Lydia lived in Spain, which was why Constance was aboard the *Octavia* at that very moment, but the distance was not the only challenge. Papa still blamed her aunt for her mother's death eleven years earlier. He wanted nothing more to do with Aunt Lydia or the Claremonts after the vessel transporting Constance and her mother to Spain had been attacked and sunk by pirates. Constance had survived, but the pirates had kidnapped her and held her for ransom.

Nevertheless, desperation sometimes called for harsh measures. Constance was a lady, the daughter of a proud duke who happened to be destitute, though certainly not by his own design. Someone had tricked him into speculation, and she was determined to salvage her father's good name, even if it meant facing her greatest fear: drowning at sea as her mother had.

The reality of how far her family had fallen in such a short time hit Constance full force when a shrill whistle sliced over the *Octavia's* deck. She started as the ship recoiled and one thunderous volley after another discharged, vibrating the vessel from bow to stern. Lying in her bunk, Constance gripped its wooden edge, staring wide-eyed at the beams overhead and willing the deck above her to hold firm.

The ship's mighty timbers groaned and convulsed again, and she heard a younger version of herself shouting *Mama!* in her mind.

Tormented by the age-old spasm of fright, Constance held back the scream that was threatening to burst from her throat as an explosion rattled the vessel.

'Tis but another dream. It has to be!

But no, her eyes were open. She was awake!

Beads of sweat dewed on her skin. She knew all too well what awaited her if the *Octavia* sank. Shaking uncontrollably, she turned and looked around the cabin for her longtime governess and companion, Mrs. Mortimer. The woman had practically raised Constance ever since Papa had paid her ransom and gotten her back from the pirates, and now Morty stared back at her charge from her own bunk. They locked terrified gazes.

Thump!

Morty cried out. "What is happening?" The pale woman gasped as the handle on the bulkhead door joggled. "Are we in danger?"

Constance's anxiety increased as the would-be intruder began pounding on the sturdy cabin door. Thankfully, the bolt she'd placed over it during the night was holding fast. With a racing heart, she pushed against the hull for purchase when another loud explosion boomed overhead.

She took as deep a breath as her lungs would allow. Her uncle, Lord Simon Danbury, had assured her that merchant vessels were not typically targeted at sea, but it was possible that a French ship had gone rogue. Napoleon had recently proclaimed himself Emperor of France, and he'd enlisted the help of pirates to pillage foreign ships near its shores. France and Spain were allies now, too, making her journey to Spain even more treacherous. Of course, her uncle had informed her about this before she'd boarded the *Octavia*, but if Napoleon was sponsoring piracy . . .

Her chin quivered. She and Morty could be in mortal danger. The French were crueler than the Spaniards!

Please, God, spare us . . .

The *Octavia* had passed Quiberon and was headed deep into the heart of the Bay of Biscay. Corsairs plied their trade from Saint-Malo, to Cadiz, to Tripoli, so it was anybody's

Excerpt from Duke by Day, Rogue by Night

guess when and where—and if—they would strike. But when they did, the poor souls aboard the unfortunate vessel were oftentimes ransomed for exorbitant sums, sold into slavery on the Barbary Coast, or worse.

Thump! Thump!

"Lady Constance!" Lieutenant Henry Guffald's passionate shout filled her with dread. In the five days they'd been at sea, the lieutenant had never once sought to rouse them from their slumber. Something was terribly wrong.

Constance sat up and cast off her wool blanket, her legs shaking as her feet hit the deck. She had to find out what was going on, no matter the impropriety or the hour.

"Nay, Constance," Morty said, reaching out to stop her. "You are not properly dressed."

Constance looked down at her night rail and grimaced. Morty was right. She grabbed her robe, shoved her arms through the sleeves, and laced it at the neck just as another explosion rocked the vessel. Constance was thrown into the washstand. The porcelain bowl clanged to the ground, smashing into pieces, and the blow left a paralyzing sting against her mouth and jaw. She tasted blood and tested her teeth with her tongue; thankfully, they were still sound.

Thump! Thump! Thump!

Dabbing her mouth with her fingers, she lunged for the door and lifted the bolt.

Lieutenant Guffald swept through the portal, pushing his way past her until he was inside the cabin. "Lady Constance! Pirates have drawn alongside us and plan to board."

"Pirates?" The barely audible word rushed out of her mouth. Her horrifying nightmare had become reality.

"Yes," he confirmed. "I fear the situation is grim. I have come to warn the two of you." The lieutenant flicked a glance about the small cabin. "Stay here. Bolt the door, and admit no one until I return."

Constance opened her mouth to speak, but no words came out.

Lieutenant Guffald dragged his attention away from Constance and addressed Morty. "Mrs. Mortimer, I beg you, make sure no one enters this room but me."

Morty nodded vigorously. "We will do as you say, sir."

Another explosion rent the air, and the *Octavia* listed to port. Morty screamed, and Constance lost her balance. Lieutenant Guffald wrapped his arms about Constance to keep her from slipping to the floor. When the vessel stabilized, he immediately unhanded her and said, "I must go."

Dazed and slightly unnerved by the accidental intimacy, Constance nodded. "Thank you, Lieutenant—" she paused "—for coming to warn us."

"Aye," Morty agreed. "You are most kind."

Lieutenant Guffald's lip curled to one side, and an odd light illuminated his cerulean-blue eyes from within as his gaze settled on Constance. "*Do not* leave this cabin." He reached for her, squeezing her shoulders with his long, lean fingers. When he released her, he swept those fingers down to clasp her hand and brought it to his lips before retreating to the door. He turned and held her gaze longer than necessary. "I *will* return for you both."

"Thank you, Lieutenant," Constance said, wondering if they would ever see him again. "Godspeed."

The cabin door closed with finality, sealing them in, and the scraping of the bolt as Morty helped Constance put it in place stripped her fraught nerves. Cannon explosions deafened her ears, and she fought hard to quell her rising panic. The ship's timbers vibrated. Something hollow seemed to collide with the hull. Voices of berserkers rose in the night. Footsteps pounded above their heads; gunshots, sharp orders, and screams rang out. Constance held Morty close as the

Excerpt from Duke by Day, Rogue by Night

sounds of murder and mayhem multiplied, filling her imagination with horror.

Morty shivered and then pulled away. "Quickly, Constance. You must change into your clothes!"

"We are under attack, Morty, yet all you can think about is—"

The *Octavia* heaved again. Her timber objected, and a combination of sulfur and other indelicate odors penetrated her nostrils. Good heavens, what if the ship caught fire?

Constance snatched at Morty's arms, fighting back the terror coursing through her as her memories vied for control: Hiding behind her mother's skirts. Pirates cackling. Her mother begging. The gentle voice that had soothed all Constance's childish woes pleading—no, *arguing*—for the life of her child . . .

"No!" she cried, letting go of Morty. She grasped her head, willing the nightmarish memories to fade.

What if they killed Morty? Constance couldn't watch another woman she loved die, especially not because of her.

Constance studied the bolt barring the cabin door, knowing the wood wouldn't hold for long. If the men meant to break down the bulkhead, they would. That door was also their one and only escape from the cabin. She grabbed a handful of her hair and tried to calm her mind as men screamed out in anger or agony, she knew not which.

What was happening? Were the crew being slaughtered, or were they successfully fighting off the horde? In either case, nothing good could come from it. She had to find a way to get them out of this alive, for Morty's sake and for Papa's. She would fight, just as her mother had, and if these attackers were corsairs, perhaps she could persuade them to ransom the two of them, just as her mother had tried to do for herself and Constance.

Her shoulders sagged in defeat. What difference would

that make? Papa couldn't provide the funds. Aunt Lydia had the means, but Constance had no way to know if her letter even had reached her aunt, let alone if she would agree to help Papa.

"You must dress, Constance," Morty insisted once more, holding up a gown.

"This is no time for vanity," Constance said. "We need a weapon."

Morty began weeping. "Do you intend to make it easy for them to ravage you?"

"Zounds!" Constance stiffened and cut a worried glance at Morty. It was up to Constance to be the voice of reason now.

"We will *not* be ravaged, not if I have anything to do with it. Come. Fear cripples the mind and prevents a person from making sound decisions. We must prepare. Help me find a something we can use to protect ourselves." Her heart beat loudly in her ears. Her chest felt as if it were full of gunpowder and one breath would ignite a spark, making it explode. If they died, they wouldn't reach Spain. If they didn't reach Spain, she couldn't help Papa. If she couldn't help Papa—

"We do not have any weapons," Morty said. "Oh, what's to become of us?"

Constance stopped rummaging through a tapestry bag and glanced up. "I do not know. But if we do not make it to Spain, I fear what will become of him."

Morty sniveled as she dazedly glanced around the cabin, clutching the gown to her breast. "Who, child?"

"Papa, of course!"

"The lieutenant said he would not allow any harm to come to us. We must believe him." Morty wasn't a good liar. "As long as you are still alive, you will find a way to help your father. I know what you're capable of, Constance. If a way can be found, you will find it, and I will be beside you when you do."

The four walls of the cabin felt oppressive, as if they were closing in on them, making it harder and harder for Constance to breathe. "Do you think I'm being punished for trying to prevent my marriage to Lord Burton?"

"Punished? Fate does not rule in weights and balances," Morty scolded. Casting aside the gown, she lifted a green pelisse off the deck. "Here. Put this on. If you will not allow me to help you with a gown, this will brace the chill and provide some degree of modesty at least." She held out the long coat.

Constance peered at the beams overhead as an eerie silence fell. Trembling, she began to thread one of her arms through one of the sleeves. Had Lieutenant Guffald and Captain Collins won?

Get Duke by Day, Rogue by Night now!

Made in the USA
Columbia, SC
24 February 2019